READY, AIM ... MURDER

They stood facing each other and now the room was entirely still.

"Draw."

Chris grabbed the gun from his waistband with a deft and sure motion and pointed it at Jamie. But Jamie's gun was already in his hand, aimed at his son's chest.

"Beat you this time."

"You did."

Jamie's laugh again filled the room, merry and exultant.

"And now, Pardner, I let you have it."

"Go ahead," Chris smiled.

And he never knew why he did it, but something within him told him to move and as he did, Jamie squeezed the trigger and there was a flash and a roar

A bullet grazed past Chris's head and thudded into the wall behind him.

Then they heard Ellen's scream.

SLOWLY, SLOWLY I RAISE THE GUN

Jay Bennett

AN AVON  FLARE BOOK

SLOWLY, SLOWLY I RAISE THE GUN is an original publication of Avon Books. This work has never before appeared in book form.

AVON BOOKS
A division of
The Hearst Corporation
1790 Broadway
New York, New York 10019

Copyright © 1983 by Jay Bennett
Published by arrangement with the author
Library of Congress Catalog Card Number: 83-45182
ISBN: 0-380-84426-5

Library of Congress Cataloging in Publication Data

Bennett, Jay.
  Slowly, slowly I raise the gun.

  (An Avon Flare book)
  Summary: Two weeks before he is due to receive his inheritance on his eighteenth birthday, Chris receives an anonymous letter informing him that his mother did not die a natural death and that he himself is in danger from the murderer.
  [1. Fathers and sons—Fiction. 2. Murder—Fiction. 3. Inheritance and succession—Fiction] I. Title.
PZ7.B4399S   1983   [Fic.]   83-45182
ISBN 0-380-84426-5

First Flare Printing, August, 1983

*Slowly, slowly I raise the gun
and point it at the head of
my father*

For
VICTORIA *and* CHRISTOPHER GORDON PRYOR
with affection

1

It all started with the letter. The slowly building terror, the desperate searching for the elusive truth, and then the great, haunting sadness that spread through him to his very soul. Yes, it all started with the letter and before it was over he knew that he had to kill.

Or be killed.

That was the only way it could finally end.

He remembered the exact time the letter came into his consciousness. The precise moment it entered his experience. He was sitting alone in his room reading with complete absorption the play *Hamlet* and he had come to the searing instant when the ghost of Hamlet's father cries out:

Revenge his foul and most unnatural murder.
Murder!

And it was when Hamlet in agony and terror whispered the word *murder,* yes it was then that Chris Gordon turned from the fevered world of the play and looked out and over to the ticking clock on the wall.

The slender black hands showed six minutes after six o'clock.

"Six minutes after six," he said aloud.

His voice sounded thin and strange in the stillness of the room. The words hung in the air and then faded away and the silence rushed in again. He moved his gray eyes away from the old pale face of the clock and it was then that he saw the white, stark white, envelope lying flat against the dark blue of the rug.

He sat staring at the white envelope and wondering how it had come to be there. When he had entered the room a full hour ago, there was no letter on the rug. Or on his desk. Or on the couch. No letter on the bed in the arched alcove.

He looked through the open doorway to the high, shadowy hall. There was no sound of anyone in the large, silent house.

"Six minutes after six," he murmured, and did not know why he did that.

He slowly got up from his chair and went over to the envelope and stooped and picked it up. It was cold to his touch.

He read the typewritten words on the envelope.

Christopher Gordon
Gordon Estate
Country Road
Palance, New York

He carefully opened the envelope, the shadow of his tall, rangy body wavering on the far wall of the large room. Outside, the light of the late May day was beginning to fade; the leaves of the trees glowed and flickered in a soft breeze.

In the room the clock ticked and one of its slender black hands moved and stopped.

He drew out a folded sheet of white paper from the envelope. There was no letterhead. No signature.

He slowly read the typewritten words, his lips moving with each word. Moving silently.

10

Six years ago when you were a boy of twelve your mother died. Today is the day of her death. Christopher Gordon, your mother did not die a natural death.

She was murdered.

Chris closed his eyes and then opened them again.

I cannot reveal myself to you, for then, I, too, will be in danger of death. Just as you are now. For the murderer still lives.

There were no more words.

Chris felt his hands begin to shake violently and the sheet of paper dropped from his grasp to the floor. He did not pick the letter up. He went over to the couch and sat down, with a slack motion. His face had become pale and drawn. His eyes cold and distant. He stared through the long oblong window at the tops of the trees and at the vast and deep sky above them.

He saw nothing.

But he remembered everything.

Yes, she did die six years ago. On this very day. They told him she had died of cancer. The headmaster of the school had called him into his office and...

She had died a peaceful death in this very house. Down below in the west wing. Died in the house that had been in her family, the Bentley family, for over three generations. The house that his father had completely renovated when he remarried a year ago.

Chris remembered the funeral, the long endless gray day, remembered standing next to his father, who kept his head bowed and averted all through the dismal ceremony. He was a silent giant of a man, his big hand holding the smaller hand of Chris, but he never said a single word to him, and then Chris remembered Aunt Rhoda Bentley gently drawing

11

Chris away from him and saying, She was glad to go, Chris. It was a release for her.

Her eyes gleamed when she spoke. Her voice was calm and consoling but her eyes, always so clear and controlled, now gleamed with a repressed and savage intensity.

Rhoda Bentley, his mother's only sister. There had been no brothers.

A peaceful death, he thought bitterly.

The clock kept ticking on and the slender black hand moved and stopped.

A peaceful death.

He got up and went over to the paper and picked it up and looked at the words again. For an instant they shimmered and the only word that remained clear and sharp and cold was the word *murdered*.

Murdered.

He crumpled the paper in his closing fist and went over to the window and looked out at the serene sky, the trees clustering about the house, and then he saw the spread of smooth grass and beyond that the tall stand of elm trees that went down to the small glistening lake.

Glistening with a faint pinkish glow.

His mother used to like to sit by the lake with him and talk of his future. Chris remembered the last words she spoke to him.

It was the last time he saw her alive.

Your father was a great football figure, Chris. Don't go his way. Never let him influence you.

Her voice was soft and sad. And now as he looked back in memory he could see, yes, he was certain of it, a shadow of fear in her eyes.

Why didn't he see it then?

Fear, stark and pale.

He wants to make you into his lost image. To become a star like he was. To take on where he had to leave off when his career was over. Don't do it, Chris. He's a good man. And I love him dearly. But don't go his way. It's not the life for you. Believe me. We have different values. Different ways of looking at life, Chris. We are Bentleys. Always remember that.

Bentleys.

The word echoed and faded and then her soft, sad voice vanished.

Chris breathed in deeply and then turned away from the window, away from the view of the glistening lake. His lips were tight. He sat down at his desk again, smoothed out the paper and carefully put it back into the envelope. He studied the postmark on the face of the envelope.

Seaside, New York.

He knew no one in Seaside. Had never been there. It was a small fishing village out on Long Island. A distance from the city. He remembered his mother telling him that she used to go there a few summers before she married Jamie Gordon.

Christopher Gordon sat a little longer in his room, listening to the relentless ticking of the clock and watching the slender black hand move and stop, move and stop. Then suddenly he stirred himself and rose. He put on his jacket, slid the envelope into the inner pocket, and then turned out the light over his desk. The room filled with gentle shadows and half-lights.

He stood there motionless, thinking, ever thinking.

He went out of the room and down one flight of steps and then down another and was now in the spacious foyer of the house. He stood there a moment, tall and hesitant, and then he turned into a hallway, walked along it, his steps noiseless on the thick carpet, and finally he stopped at an oak-paneled door. He tried the gold knob and the door swung open.

He stepped into a shadowy room that had a high ceiling lined with parallel oak beams. The curtains at the high, narrow windows were drawn. He looked about him for his father but Jamie Gordon was not

13

sitting in his black leather chair, his massive hands caressing the burnished stock of one of his favorite antique shotguns.

The room was empty.

Chris stood there, alone in the stillness, gazing about him, a quiet hard look in his gray eyes. He scanned the gleaming gold trophies lining the shelves, the framed photographs on the walls, the letters from two presidents of the United States, the gun racks, and then the shatterproof glass gun cases with their collection of handguns.

The cases were locked.

All the windows of the room had bars to them.

Chris thought grimly how much his father loved guns, guns of all kinds and of all provenances, and how much his mother had hated them. How bitter she was at the times Jamie took his son hunting or out to the range for target practice. Only after she was dead and gone out of the house did Jamie build for himself this trophy room. When she was alive all was kept in a separate small building far from the main house.

Chris stood there remembering that his mother had never set foot into that wooden building.

He turned abruptly and left the room, shutting the door behind him. He took out his key case, found the right key, and then locked the door.

He went down another hallway and walked through a vast living room, bright and modern, and out onto a flagstone terrace. His father was lounging in a metal patio chair, watching a baseball game on television.

He raised one of his big hands and motioned to a chair.

"Sit down, Chris. The Yanks are winning."

Chris nodded silently and sat down.

"Make yourself a drink."

Jamie Gordon was drinking Scotch on the rocks.

14

Chris could see by the red crayon line on the bottle that he had gone over his quota for the day.

"No, thanks."

Jamie glanced at him and smiled.

"You learn to drink early and it will never throw you, Chris. It never threw me. Never missed a game. My daddy taught me early."

He motioned to a movable bar that stood close to them.

"Lay off, Jamie," Chris said quietly.

A cold glitter came into Jamie's eyes and then it went away and he was smiling again.

"Okay," he murmured.

He was a huge smiling man with large black eyes; black hair, thick and wavy; a large face with clear features, clear and rugged. It was an open and very likable face, Chris thought, sitting back and almost coldly studying his father. Jamie still kept himself in condition. Just ten pounds over his playing weight of two hundred and sixty.

He was six feet five.

"Okay, Chris," Jamie said mildly. "Just trying to be sociable."

Chris took after his mother's family. He was blond and fair-skinned. Just close to six feet with a lean and rangy body.

He had his mother's good looks.

Small, delicately shaped features. Soft gray eyes. A gentle smile. This was all his mother's.

He moved with the easy grace of the born athlete. And this was his father's gift.

You'd make an All Pro tight end, Jamie had said time and again. Your reflexes are better than mine ever were. You're strong. Very strong. You have steel in that body of yours. Lean steel. You're a natural. A super natural, Chris.

Why don't you give me a chance, Chris? Why don't you let me try?

"You tried," Chris said aloud.

"And I struck out."

"You know damn well I don't like to see you drinking."

"I know," Jamie said. "But you always smile and let it go. I'm a big man and a big man can take a lot of liquor in his big body and..."

"Shut up, Jamie," Chris said. "Just shut up and watch your game and drink. Drink your guts out."

Jamie's hand tightened over his glass and then it relaxed.

"You're on a short string today, Chris."

"Maybe I am."

"What's the matter?"

"My mother died today."

Jamie's head went back as if Chris had slapped him. He breathed in slowly and then relaxed again. The color came back into his face.

"Today six years ago," he said in a flat voice.

"It was like it was today," Chris said.

"I don't understand what you're getting at."

"You've been drinking too much to understand."

"Cut it, Chris."

"You cut it."

Jamie slowly but gracefully got up from his chair. He still has it, Chris thought. They used to call him The Big Cat. He still has that awesome flowing movement. That lithe power. Big as he is.

"You're a big man, Jamie," Chris said, still sitting in his chair and gazing up at his father. "That's all you are. A big man."

"What the hell's eating you today?"

"Nothing. Nothing at all."

"Are you challenging me? Trying to get a rise out of me?"

"Maybe I am."

"Why?"

"Who knows why, Jamie? Life is full of mysteries these days. People die. People live. And you drink."

Jamie moved forward a full step and loomed over his son.

"Don't crowd me, Chris."

"Just sit down and pour yourself another one."

"Chris."

Jamie's massive hands clenched and then gradually unclenched. There were little beads of sweat on his forehead. He stared hard at his son and then slowly sat down again.

There was a silence.

And Chris, looking across at him, thought with a sadness, How proud I was of you all through my growing years. You were a national celebrity. Two presidents invited you to the White House. And you took me along. You were always on the sports pages of the country. All Pro middle linebacker ten times. Super Bowl winner four times. The heart of a team that won all its games two seasons running. And when you had to quit football that team was through. It never found its way back to a championship.

You were its heart and I was so proud of you.

Jamie Gordon's only son.

Everybody loved me because of you. You made everything easy for me. School, girls; everywhere I went you made things easy for me. People bent over backward to do things for me.

Because of you, Jamie.

It was a great feeling. And yet underneath it all I know now, now at this moment, that I feared you.

Would you believe it, my father? I feared you.

And still do.

"Jamie," he heard himself say.

"Yes?"

Jamie's voice was harsh.

"When you played they always said you were the fiercest hitter in the history of pro football."

"They said that," Jamie muttered.

"You'd hit a man and he'd go down and stay down."

"If I hit him right."

"If you hit him right," Chris echoed softly.

"So?"

"Tell me."

"Tell you what?"

There was a bewildered look in Jamie's black eyes.

"Did you ever think this way?"

"What way?" Jamie's voice rose. "What way?"

Chris leaned forward and looked squarely at his father.

"Did you ever stop to think that you might hit a man hard enough to kill him?"

"Kill him?"

"Yes."

"I don't get you."

"Just think about it a minute. You'll get it."

And Chris could swear, watching the play of thought and emotion on Jamie's clear face, that not once, no, not once in his entire playing career did his father ever consider the question.

A breeze came up and ruffled Jamie's black hair and then all was quiet and calm again. Chris waited.

"It's the game, Chris," Jamie finally said. "The game. You're supposed to hit him as hard as you can."

"And if he died?"

"Then he dies."

"It's a form of murder, wouldn't you say, Jamie?"

"Murder? What are you talking about?"

"Well, isn't it?"

Jamie shook his head fiercely.

"No, Chris. It's the game. The game."

Chris smiled bitterly.

"I thought you would say that."

"Why?"

But Chris didn't answer him.

"And life is a game, too, isn't it, Jamie?"

"Life?"

"Yes, Jamie. Life."

He sat there waiting for his father to answer. But he knew it already.

"Well?"

"I...I guess so. Yes, it is."

"You didn't disappoint me, Jamie," Chris said quietly.

"What do you mean?"

"Nothing."

Jamie ran his massive hand through his dark hair again and again and then he spoke.

"I can't make you out today, Chris. I can't."

"I can't either."

"What do you mean by that?"

"Let it be, Jamie," Chris said wearily and got up.

He saw Ellen, Jamie's wife, come to the threshold of the terrace and stand there gazing at them. There was a concerned, almost poignant, look on her face.

It touched him.

He had liked Ellen from the moment Jamie brought her home. He was all prepared to hate her but he found himself liking her.

And she became his good friend.

She was a tall and very pretty woman with dark brown hair and luminous brown eyes. A frank and warm person who always showed genuine feeling for him. Jamie had met her in a restaurant in Chicago.

She had been a waitress there.

"You going?"

"Yes, Jamie. I'm going. By the way, you left the gun house unlocked."

"It's the trophy room," Jamie said harshly.

And Chris didn't know why he was baiting Jamie so much. He knew he had touched a sore point with Jamie. His mother always called the small wooden building where Jamie kept his trophies and guns the gun house. Called it that with contempt in her voice. And Jamie had always gritted his teeth when she had said that.

"You know it's the trophy room," Jamie said again.

19

"Call it whatever the hell you want but keep it locked," Chris said with the same contempt in his voice that his mother had always used. "Guns kill people and other living beings."

She had always said that. Her voice soft but cutting. Oh, so cutting.

Guns kill people. And other living beings.

Jamie's eyes blazed. But this time he kept himself under complete control. He did not rise from his seat.

"I said you were on a short string today."

"You called it right."

"Why, Chris?"

And now he could see that Jamie was carefully studying him. Very carefully.

"I told you why. My mother died today."

Jamie shook his head grimly.

"It's not that at all."

"It's your drinking."

"No. What is it, Chris?"

They looked at each other in cold silence.

"Let it be," Chris finally said.

He walked slowly to where Ellen stood.

"What's wrong, Chris?" she murmured.

Chris smiled gently at her.

"It's all okay."

"Are you sure?"

"Sure."

She looked to where Jamie sat staring at the drink in his hand, his face a taut mask.

"When he first got up from his chair, I thought he was going to hit you, Chris. I was watching the two of you from the living room. But I couldn't hear what you were saying to each other."

"We were just talking."

She shook her head.

"I really thought he was going to do it, Chris."

"Did you?"

"Yes. I got cold as ice all over."

"He never hit me in all my life, Ellen."

20

"I was scared then."

"You shouldn't have been. You don't know him as well as I do."

"I think I know him. What did you say to get him so worked up?"

He didn't answer her.

"What, Chris?"

"Let it alone, Ellen," he said gently.

She touched his face tenderly. Her fingers were cold, cold as ice. And he wondered if she, too, had come to fear his father.

"Don't crowd him, Chris. He's got a lot on his mind these days."

"I guess he has," Chris said curtly.

"Please, Chris."

"Okay. I'll keep my distance." He smiled at her.

He went past Ellen and through the living room and into the foyer and then he turned and saw that she had followed him.

Quietly.

Silently.

"Chris?"

"Yes?"

"Are you going to be home late?"

"I don't know," he said.

"A date?"

"I'm going into the city to see my Aunt Rhoda."

"Oh," she said.

Rhoda and Ellen did not care for each other.

"I might stay over. I might come back."

He was about to turn when she stopped him.

"Did you get the letter?"

"Letter?"

He had paled.

His hand went instinctively to the inner pocket of his jacket and then came away from it with a guilty motion.

And then he realized that he had begun to tremble.

He clenched his fist hard and the trembling left him. But he was certain that she had seen it all.

He heard her voice as from a distance.

"It was out in the mailbox," she said. "So I took it and brought it up to your room."

"When?"

"Oh, about an hour ago. I saw you studying and I didn't want to disturb you. You didn't seem to hear me."

"I didn't hear you come in or go out," he said.

She smiled and looked gently at him and he thought to himself, How very pretty you are, Ellen. How close I feel to you now.

No longer fearful and alone.

"That's the way I wanted it, Chris. I dropped the letter on the rug. Just behind your chair. I was sure you'd see it."

"I saw it, Ellen."

"Anything important?"

She had said the words casually but he felt her eyes probing into him. There seemed to be fear and anxiety in them. Fear and anxiety for him.

For an instant he wanted to open up and tell her. To take out the letter and show it to her.

His lips were about to speak.

"No," he heard himself say.

"I thought it might be. For some reason the letter was delivered after all the regular mail. That's why I thought to bring it up to you."

"It was not important," he said abruptly.

He turned and went out of the house and into the shadows. A lone departing figure. His footsteps scraped along the gravel driveway that led to the fieldstone garage. He opened one of the wooden doors and it grated in the silence. His finger caught on a nail and he felt a sharp sting and then saw the tiny drops of blood.

Shining darkly.

He thought of his mother.

Murdered.

Ellen stood in the house a long time, gazing after him. Only when she heard the sound of his car fading into the twilight did she turn away.

Out on the darkening terrace Jamie Gordon took another drink. There was a haunted, desperate look in his black eyes.

2

He drove along the highway and soon darkness came down ánd the lights of cars flashed by him. But all he saw was the blackness of the night. And all he heard again and again in the rhythm of the spinning wheels, like a mad, mad song was:

> Did they kill you,
>   Mother, Mother?
> Did they kill you,
>   Mother, Mother?
> Did they shed your blood,
>   Mother, Mother?
> Did they shed your blood,
>   Your blood,
>   Your blood,
>   Your blood...

Till he had to pull over and thrust his hands to his ears to blot out the sound. It was then that he called his Aunt Rhoda and found that she was still in her apartment. She was about to go out to the theater. He asked her to stay home and spend the evening with him. She asked him why. But he didn't tell her the true reason.

Just laughed it off and said he had been wanting

to see her, for days on end. To see his beautiful Aunt Rhoda.

He got back into the car and started off again. A soft peace settled over him. And then he asked himself, Why didn't I call her from the house? Before I started out? I told Ellen I was going there and I didn't even know if Rhoda would be in.

Why was I so certain that Rhoda would be home?

And then he said to himself, Because this night is different from all the other nights in my life. She had to be in. On this night of all nights.

Fate decreed it so.

We are all creatures of fate.

He laughed out loud.

And then he stopped laughing and thought wistfully, I shall go mad before it is all over.

Like poor Hamlet.

I shall go mad.

3

He was standing admiring the Renoir, forgetting everything but the beauty and the serenity of the painting, the world of blood and death blotted out, when he heard her voice behind him.

"You've always liked that painting."

"Yes, Rhoda," he said without turning.

Her voice warmed him. It was good to be with her.

"That is one of the best he ever did in that genre. I've lent it out to museums all over the world."

"It's priceless," he murmured.

"Oh, nothing's priceless these days, Chris. I guess it would go for a million or so."

"You're surely not planning to sell it, Rhoda?"

"No. I wouldn't sell it."

He looked at the painting again and shrugged almost despairingly.

"I don't know why. I just can't figure it out. But from the minute I saw this Renoir I sort of fell in love with it. I must've been all of six years old."

"You do have a fine taste for art, Chris. And this is a beauty. But what about the Picassos and the Matisses and the Pissarros and the..."

He shook his head and she smiled tolerantly and stopped speaking.

"You've a great collection, Rhoda. They say it's one of the best collections in the east."

"Only in the east," she smiled. "Of modern art. Private. Outside of museums."

"But this is my favorite of them all," he said.

She nodded tenderly and then moved back a bit and studied him.

"You're absolutely sure?"

"No doubt in my mind."

And he thought, How peaceful and settling it is to be here with Rhoda and talk of paintings and feel the goodness of people to each other and not to think of...

Death.

Death, cold and bloody.

She nodded again and moved closer to him.

"Then my mind's made up."

"About what?"

But she didn't answer him.

"Bend your head," she said.

"Why?"

"Because you're so much taller than I am. Now do it."

He bent his head to her.

"Now kiss your old Aunt Rhoda."

"Old?"

"Do it."

He laughed and kissed her.

"That's a good nephew."

"Your only nephew."

"My only one," she murmured.

She held him and then released him. Her eyes sparkled and at that moment she reminded him so very much of his mother.

They used to be taken for twins. But Rhoda was the older of the two.

"I've just decided to give you this Renoir for your wedding present," she said.

"Give me?"

He stared at her.

"You do have a girl, don't you?"

"A few."

"No special ones?"

"Well, maybe one."

"What's her name?"

"Lisa. Lisa Andrews."

"That's a pretty name for a pretty girl. She is pretty?"

"Yes. What's this about giving me the painting?"

"Blond like you? Or dark?"

"Dark."

"Good. Opposites make for good relationships."

"I guess we like each other. We get along pretty well."

Rhoda sighed gently.

"That's pleasant to hear. I'm sure you do things together."

He nodded.

"We're both in the school graduation play. I'm Hamlet and she's Ophelia."

"Oh?"

And before she could speak again he said, "Now, Rhoda, I don't know when I'm getting married. It could be ten years from now. It could be never. But I do know I'm not taking a million-dollar painting from you."

"When is the play opening? I must come and see you."

"I'll let you know."

She gazed at him tenderly and he felt all her love for him.

"You'll make a very appealing Hamlet. How do the girls put up with your handsomeness? I would positively swoon."

"Cut it, Rhoda," he said.

"I'm embarrassing you."

"You're talking silly."

She reached up and touched his soft blond hair, her fingers stroking it.

"But you make me silly. You bring back the days of my golden youth. Of joy. Of love..." Her voice faltered and then thinned. "Of...love...and...heart ...break..."

Her eyes darkened and her voice faded away. Her delicate hands trembled and were still.

"Rhoda," he said gently.

She didn't seem to hear him.

"But Hamlet rejects Ophelia, doesn't he?" she said in a very quiet voice.

The lightness and the gaiety were gone out of her.

"She goes mad," he said.

Rhoda slowly nodded.

"Yes. She goes mad."

And he felt a coldness come subtly into the room. Come in and settle there. The warm peace and serenity were being swept away.

"Because of what he did to her, Chris," she said.

A sadness had fallen over her, like a shadow.

"People can be very cruel to each other, Christopher. Especially when they claim to be in love. Especially then."

Cruel enough to kill, he thought.

"Savagely cruel, Christopher," she said, and her words were like a gleaming knife.

He looked frantically away from her to the Renoir with its glowing, lush colors, its paean to life, and then he heard her voice.

"Don't do it, Chris," she said. "Don't make my mistake and..." She stopped and seemed to catch her breath in pain and then she went on. "Marry when you're young and in love. Marry and take this Renoir out of my house. It belongs to you, Chris. To youth. Not to me."

He didn't speak.

But he wanted to say, What mistake did you make, Rhoda? Who were you so desperately in love with?

Why didn't you ever marry?

You with your wealth, your fine tastes, your beauty, your...

"Marry when you're young, Chris," she murmured. "Life without fulfilled love is a bitter death. A death."

And then he said the inner words, fierce and clear:

Who was your murderer, Rhoda?

We all have murderers in our lives, don't we?

Sooner or later we meet our murderers.

There is no escaping them.

Just as my mother could not escape hers.

"You have such a strange look on your face, Chris."

"Do I?"

"Almost as if you were about to cry."

Yes, Rhoda. To cry.

"I just thought of something, that's all."

"Did I say anything wrong? Something to upset you?"

"No, Rhoda."

He went over to a chair and sat down. She stood there in the center of the large and spacious room and gazed across at him.

The Renoir glowed behind her.

"Something is wrong," she said.

He was silent.

"You phoned and said you wanted to see me. I didn't think much of it then. But now I know something is troubling you. Greatly, Chris."

"I...I just wanted to see you, Rhoda."

"And?"

"To ask you some questions."

"About what?"

He didn't speak.

"What is it, Chris?" she asked.

"Mother died today," he said. "Six years ago."

"Yes, Chris," she said. "I'm well aware of that."

She slowly sat down on one of the couches. And

for the first time he could see Rhoda Bentley as she would be in old age.

Her smooth copper hair seemed to darken. The fair, delicate face with the small, placid blue eyes became dim and cold. The young lithe figure became slack and fragile.

"I want to talk about her. And about my father," he said.

"I wish you wouldn't, Chris," she said without looking up.

She sat there in silence, vulnerable and alone.

"I have to," he said.

"Why?"

And he wanted to shout at her in his agony, Someone killed her. Murdered her. And now may want to murder me.

But he sat there saying nothing.

"Why?" she asked again, and this time she straightened up and her eyes were small and hard.

His hand went to his inner pocket and came away empty.

This is the second time I have made that exact motion tonight, he thought. The second time to people I have always trusted.

"Chris, answer me."

And suddenly he knew that he was now forever alone and isolated. With the coming of the letter he had been cut adrift from all people. He could trust no one anymore.

No one.

Not even Rhoda, who was going to give him a million-dollar painting.

You're beginning to think and act like Hamlet, he said to himself. He trusted nobody but his good friend Horatio. And at crucial times, not even him.

He took the lone road.

Because he had to.

To survive.

"Chris," she said again in a sharp voice.

31

He looked squarely at her.

"I've been thinking about my mother, Rhoda," he said. "And about the way she died."

Rhoda paled.

"What do you mean by that?"

"How did she really die?"

"Really? What do you mean by that word?"

"You once told me that she died a peaceful death."

"Yes. I said that."

"Did she?"

Her face now had a gray pallor to it. Her lips slightly quivered as she spoke.

"Why are you doubting me, Chris?"

"I'm not doubting you. I told you I've been doing a lot of thinking."

"Recently?"

She was watching him warily. Just as his father had on the terrace.

"As recently as today."

"Today," she echoed.

"Yes, Rhoda."

"Any special reason other than that this is the anniversary of Marian's death? Well, Chris?"

And as she said that, the thought flared through his mind, Maybe it was Rhoda who sent me the letter?

"No," he said.

She drew in her breath and then began to speak.

"Chris, your mother had cancer. She lingered and then she died painlessly and quite peacefully."

"Were you there?"

"I was downstairs in the big living room. The one in the west wing."

"Who was with her?"

"Chris, what is this all about?"

"Please tell me."

"Your father was alone with her when it happened."

"Ah," he sighed low and was silent.

She kept watching him.

"You seem to be in a very strange mood tonight, Chris."

"Maybe I am."

"I've never seen you this way before. Did you have a quarrel with your father?"

"No."

"You did, Chris. Keep out of his way. He can be a violent man."

"I can handle him."

"Keep out of his way."

"Tell me, Rhoda," Chris said grimly.

"Yes?"

"You saw her face?"

"Her face?"

"It was peaceful?"

She hesitated before she spoke. He wondered if she was telling him the truth.

"Yes, Chris," she said. "Quite peaceful. Jamie came down to tell me and I went up immediately. She lay there quiet and serene. As if she were sleeping."

As if she were sleeping, he thought sardonically. Rhoda, what do you really know?

"Sleeping. Are you sure, Rhoda?"

"Why are you doubting me?"

"I'm in a doubting mood tonight, Rhoda," he said.

"Then clear away your doubts, once and for all. Marian died a peaceful death," Rhoda said in a flat voice.

Yet, he thought bitterly, her eyes are quietly, oh so quietly, studying me. Trying to probe through to my center. The same way Jamie did when we sat on the terrace together and I began to crowd him.

Don't crowd me, Chris.

And I crowded him.

Am I crowding Rhoda now? Does she know more than she wants to tell me?

Is she, too, fearful for her life?

"Has Jamie money?" he suddenly asked.

33

"I don't know."

"He's supposed to own a piece of the Tigers football team. Is that true?"

"I know nothing about Jamie Gordon's money."

"Please tell me, Rhoda."

"Chris, confide in me. What is really troubling you tonight? What is at the bottom of these questions?"

He shook his head grimly.

"Tell me what you know about his money."

She stared long at him and then she sighed low and began to speak.

"When his career ended he wanted to buy into a major football team. But he didn't have the money."

"And?"

"He came to your mother and asked her for it."

"What did she do?"

"Let me first tell you this. Jamie Gordon married into wealth. Your mother and I were the only heirs to your grandfather's fortune. A very considerable one."

"And Mother wouldn't give him the money?"

Rhoda's eyes glinted with satisfaction.

"Not a cent."

"Not a cent," he echoed softly.

And Jamie's face rose up before him, bitter and dark.

He heard his aunt speak again.

"I know they quarreled bitterly over that. It was a matter of six million dollars, Chris."

"As much as that?"

"Yes. And Jamie Gordon didn't have that kind of money."

"So he couldn't buy into the team?"

She didn't immediately answer him. He waited.

"A year after Marian's death I learned that he was well able to," she said quietly.

"How did he get the money?"

She hesitated.

34

"How, Rhoda?"

"You'd better ask George Ramsey. Our family lawyer. He could tell you."

"And you can't?"

She shook her head.

"He wouldn't tell me. But he might have reasons for telling you."

"What reasons?"

"I don't know. Speak to him."

And then there was silence in the room.

Chris sat there, thinking, ever thinking, and suddenly he became aware that she was standing over him.

He slowly looked up at her.

Her body was rigid. Her face quiet and intense.

"Christopher."

"Yes?"

"Leave that house."

"What?"

"Leave it. Damn it, leave the house."

"Rhoda."

"Do as I tell you."

He stared up at her and her face now had the same savage repressed fury that he saw in it when she stood by him at his mother's grave.

"Come live with me. Why do you want to go on living with a football player and a waitress in a small town in Westchester? Why?"

He kept staring up at her and as he did he felt a chill slowly settle within him.

"Life is here, Chris. Get away from him as fast as you can. He's no good for you. He's a big, overgrown, spoiled, witless child. When he doesn't get what he wants, he becomes violent and deadly. Get away from him."

"He's my father," Chris said in a very low voice.

"He's your father," Rhoda said bitterly. "I wish to God she never saw him. Never met him. Marian fell in love with a body. A body."

"Rhoda," Chris said and stood up.

But she didn't seem to be aware of him.

"She was such a fool. Such a young fool. Just wanted her hands on a beautiful body. A body."

"Rhoda, stop it," Chris said.

But she went on.

"Such a fool. Such a young, passionate fool. A girl who had no shame. No dignity. No..."

"Rhoda," Chris shouted.

She stood there and shivered.

Large tears came to her eyes.

"Chris."

And now she was fully aware of him.

"Chris," she said again and her voice broke.

She thrust out her hands and grabbed him to her.

"Forgive me. I didn't mean to speak of Marian that way. I loved her with all my heart. You know that, Chris. You know that. I'm not myself today. The day brings back such terrible memories. Such terrible ones."

"What terrible memories?" he asked fiercely.

But she didn't answer him.

"Chris, I need you. I need you. Come live with me. With me."

"Tell me."

"Come live with me. With me."

And she began to weep and would not let him go.

4

He put the car into the garage next to the other cars, turned out the lights, and then softly closed the big wooden doors. He stepped out and onto the gravel driveway, his footsteps scraping along in the vast silence of the night. He walked on, footsteps scraping the gravel rhythmically, and then he saw the figure of Jamie looming near the house.

He shivered and then stopped.

"Chris?"

Jamie's voice floated over to him.

"Yes, Jamie."

He began walking again to the house. It was close to three o'clock in the morning and the sky had a sliver of a pale moon and scudding dark clouds.

There was light and shadow on the gravel path.

He was now close to his father.

"Ellen said you went into the city."

"That's right."

"To Rhoda?"

"Yes."

Jamie stood on the top step and Chris stood below him, leaning against the stairway railing.

The front door was open and Chris could see the lights of the foyer. The rest of the large house was dark.

"How is Rhoda?"

"All right."

"Haven't seen her in a long while."

"She's a busy woman, Jamie."

"Yes. She is."

They spoke in low, clear voices.

"She send her regards?"

"No, Jamie. She didn't. Did you expect her to?"

"No."

Chris smiled grimly in the darkness.

"What did you talk about?"

"Paintings."

"Oh."

"We both love them, Jamie. Most civilized people do."

"I guess they do."

And you don't. You're a Neanderthal. With guns and football. A Neanderthal.

"Paintings and music. Things you know very little of, Jamie."

He knew he was lashing out at his father. Baiting him again. But the huge silent figure on the top of the steps just stood there, impassive and poised.

"Then you had a pleasant time?"

"I always do with Rhoda," Chris said. "She's my mother's only sister."

"That's right. She is," Jamie said quietly.

There was a silence.

A cloud moved across the moon like a large dark hand and there was a brief darkness and then it became lighter again.

"Why didn't you stay over? And drive back in the morning?"

"I wanted to come home, Jamie," Chris said.

Again, the silence.

Far out on the main road, the light of a car flashed through the darkness and then was gone from sight.

"Chris."

"Well?"

"What's bugging you?"

"Nothing, Jamie."

"You crowded me. Why?"

"When?"

"This evening. You know when."

"Oh."

"Well?"

"I'm your son, Jamie," Chris said sardonically. "I like to challenge people. Gets my juices going."

"You're my son," Jamie said softly.

"Your only one."

"That's right. And I'm your father. Your only one."

"I'm trying hard to remember that," Chris said.

"What do you mean by that one?"

"I'm going to sleep," Chris said abruptly.

He went up the steps and past the huge, quiet figure and into the house. Then he turned and realized that Jamie had followed him in silently.

Like a big cat.

They stood together in the lit foyer. It was then that he saw the gun stuck in the waistband of his father's jeans.

The pearl handle glinted in the light.

It unnerved him.

"What the hell is that for, Jamie?" he said fiercely.

His voice was high and tight.

"The gun?"

"Yes, damn it."

Jamie smiled easily.

"You've seen me wear a gun before."

Chris didn't speak. He slowly grabbed control of himself.

He heard his father's voice.

"Many times, Chris. Especially at night. I like the feel of it at night when I walk around the grounds."

"Yes," Chris breathed out. "I've seen you."

"So what's the big deal now?"

"Nothing."

Chris turned to go up the staircase but Jamie put his massive hand out and gently stopped him.

The fingers closed over Chris's arm.

"Tell me."

"Let go, Jamie," Chris said evenly. And then he said it again.

"Okay."

Jamie let go of his arm.

"Tell you what?" Chris asked coldly.

"Why are you suddenly so flaky about guns? You're damn good with them yourself. You're a better shot than I am. And I'm considered pretty good."

"You're pretty good."

Jamie's big black eyes were probing him.

"So?"

"So I never did care for them too much. I'm like my mother."

Jamie smiled.

"But you're also like your father. You've got a lot of me in you, Chris. My steel. My toughness."

Your violence, Father? Do I have that, too?

"You're very good with guns, Chris. You're a natural."

"Guns kill people and other living beings," Chris said.

Jamie still smiled.

"She said that."

"She did. Time and again to you. But it was like talking to a block of wood."

"Maybe it was. But I saw you bring down a deer with a damned good shot."

Chris flinched and paled.

"Yes. You did see me."

"You yelled out. You were happy. I saw you kill other things, Chris."

"You did."

"Living beings."

"I killed them."

"So?"

40

"So that's the last time you'll ever see it."

"Why?"

Chris moved closer to Jamie.

"Maybe I'm starting to go all the way with her, Jamie. I'm beginning to hate every gun in this world."

"Why?" Jamie asked again, this time very softly.

"I'll write a book on it and let you read it."

"Do that."

Chris looked up into the impassive face of his father and suddenly lashed out bitterly.

"Do you still read anymore, Jamie? Are you able to read anymore? Or do you just sit by the idiot box and watch sports and drink yourself cockeyed?"

"You're crowding me again, Chris," Jamie said in a flat voice.

"You went to college. You even graduated. What the hell did they teach you there? Football signals?"

Jamie's big hand went up.

"I said you're crowding me again."

"You just crowded me."

Jamie's hand slowly went down to his side and unclenched. They stood there facing each other in a tense stillness.

"Where's Ellen?" Chris asked quietly.

"Asleep."

"My stepmother sleeps well."

"Yes, Chris. She sleeps well."

"And you couldn't sleep?"

"No, Chris."

And Chris wanted to shout:

Why, Jamie? What's on your conscience that keeps you from sleeping?

"Good night, Jamie," he said.

Jamie didn't speak.

Chris went up the staircase, leaving his father standing alone in the foyer. When he turned at the landing and looked down, Jamie was still standing there.

His figure cast a massive shadow over the lower steps of the staircase.

Why can't you sleep, my father?

And Chris went farther up into the darkness.

5

That night he slept a restless, tossing sleep and then suddenly he felt himself waking up and gliding out of bed silently and coming to the window and looking out. A pale, wavering strip of moonlight lay across the branches and leaves of the trees.

Pale and silvery.

All about him was an unearthly stillness.

He stood there, wondering what had wakened him and what had made him go directly to the window and look out.

Then he heard a soft, rustling sound.

Almost like a soft wind.

He felt a chill come over his body as if the sound were rustling over him, cold, ever so cold.

Then he saw a white figure glide into his view. It came to a rest under the cover of one of the large trees and he could barely make out its form.

It stood there, never moving.

A still, white, shimmering figure.

Gradually he was able to make out its white, diaphanous gown and the smooth coppery hair that glistened in the moonlight.

Glistened in muted flashes of silver and gold.

The face was half-turned away from him and he could not make out its features.

Then suddenly he whispered.

"Rhoda."

But even as he said that, he knew that he was mistaken. For the figure turned its face slowly and steadily to him and now he shivered.

Violently.

Now he was certain.

"Mother," he cried out low.

And then he heard his voice again.

"Mother!"

The figure raised its hand and beckoned to him. It was then that he saw the stream of blood dripping from the delicate fingers.

A rage and fear swept over him and he was about to turn and rush down the flight of stairs and out to her side when she turned as if startled and glided back into the trees and vanished.

"Mother, come back," he pleaded.

Come back, come back...

His eyes opened and he was sitting in bed, cold, cold and still, and he knew that he had been dreaming.

And that his mother would never come back to him.

Never.

6

He put down the playscript and looked across at her. They were sitting at a small table and overhead a single light bulb glowed. There was no one else on the stage with them. The auditorium was empty and dark.

The rest of the cast had not yet come for the rehearsal.

"Chris, why did you stop?" Lisa asked.

"I...I just thought of something, that's all."

"Could you go on?"

"Sure."

She smiled at him.

"I'd like to go over the scene again before the others come. I'm still a little shaky with it."

"I understand."

"Let's go."

But he didn't pick up the playscript. Just kept gazing across at her. And thinking of the words he had just read aloud from the play.

Are you honest, Ophelia?

And he wondered if he could open up to Lisa. Could he tell her of the letter? Of his dread fears and suspicions?

Could he stand before her and say, Help me. I'm so alone, Lisa. So alone and so lost.

I just can't make it alone.

It's getting too much to bear.

Are you honest, Ophelia?

Hamlet asked that question with so much agony in his heart. He wanted to tell her and then he decided that he could not trust Ophelia.

Even though he loved her.

Are you honest, Ophelia?

Can I trust you, Lisa?

Can I?

"Chris."

"Yes."

"You're just not with the play today, are you?"

He didn't answer.

"I could feel it the minute you sat down at this table," she said gently.

"I've got something on my mind, Lisa," he said.

"What is it, Chris?"

Her voice was soft and warm. It reached into him and stirred him.

"Lisa," he whispered.

He was about to get up and go to her. But he didn't rise at all. Just sat there. Sat there and thought.

Lisa, I got a letter. And the letter shocked me, just as the ghost shocked Hamlet. The ghost tells Hamlet that his father was murdered. And the letter tells me that my mother was murdered.

Hamlet cries out:

O my prophetic soul!

He felt all along that his father's death was not a peaceful death. That something dreadful and violent had happened to his beloved father.

All along, he felt that.

Lisa, dear Lisa, I feel just like Hamlet did when he was told the shocking truth. And I say with him:

O my prophetic soul!

For somehow deep inside of me I knew that something was dreadfully wrong with my mother's death.

Deep inside of me, I never accepted it.

How well I know that now.

O my prophetic soul!

She was murdered. She was.

"Chris."

"Yes?"

"What is it?"

And looking at her, he knew how impossible it was to tell her. Hamlet was right. You go it alone.

There's no other way.

No other way in this lousy, bitter world. This world of violence and deceit. This world that's well on its way to blowing itself up. This world of blood and death.

I tell her and she's involved.

I tell her and she's in danger, too.

No, you go it alone.

Or you end up dead yourself.

He picked up the playscript.

"Let's get on with it, Lisa."

"But, Chris..."

She had risen. She was a tall girl, with long shining brown hair and a slender figure and her eyes were gentle hazel eyes.

Eyes that he had seen again and again in his memory.

And looking at her standing there, those eyes so anxious and concerned, he felt the tremendous urge to go to her and take her into his arms.

Hold her close.

Ever so close.

And then whisper to her, Lisa, Lisa, comfort me. To kiss her fragrant hair with gentle kisses.

And then whisper, Lisa, Lisa, save me from myself. I can't go it alone. I must have you with me. With me all the way.

You're the only one left.

The only one.

"Lisa," he murmured.

But he never moved from his seat.

"Chris?"

There was such a plea in her voice that he was certain she knew what was going on inside him.

He wavered for an instant and then he closed her away again.

"Let's get on with the play," he said.

"But..."

"We're losing time, Lisa. They'll soon be here."

She slowly sat down and picked up the playscript.

"Shall I take it?" he asked.

She shook her head.

"No."

And he felt she was angry at him.

"Okay."

She was about to read when she stopped and gave him a piercing look.

"What is it, Chris?"

"You've already asked that," he said.

"Have I done something wrong to you?"

"No, Lisa."

"Something weird has come over you. I can feel it."

"Then it's something weird."

"But..."

"Read your lines, will you," he said grimly.

"You take it," she said.

He nodded curtly and began to read aloud.

"Ha, ha! are you honest?"

"My lord!"

"Are you fair?"

"What means your lordship?"

And as he spoke the lines and heard her replies, he felt his heart was breaking for her.

"That if you be honest and fair, your honesty should admit no..."

He stopped mid-speech and put down the play-script and she saw that there were large tears in his eyes.

"Chris," she said and came swiftly over to him and dropped to her knees at his side.

"I'll be all right," he said.

"Yes," she murmured, her hand stroking his hair.

"I put myself too much into the play. I'll have to control it."

"Yes," she said again.

She kissed his cheek.

"Chris, please tell me."

He felt her warmth surge through him.

"Lisa."

"Please."

But suddenly he drew away from her. He wiped his eyes with the back of his hand. A grim, fierce motion.

"Let's get on with it," he said.

"Chris..."

"Come on."

She reached her hand out to him and then let it fall to her side. She went back to her chair and sat down. A silence settled over them like a gray fog. Soon the two began to read the play again while above them the single light bulb glowed bleakly.

The rest of the auditorium was dark and empty.

They read on and their voices sounded harsh and lost in the emptiness.

I'm drifting away into a dark, dark world, he thought. Drifting away and leaving her far behind me.

I'm alone.

7

"Would you care for some wine, Chris?"

"All right."

"How about a choice Chablis?"

"Good enough."

"They have some excellent wines here. Better than the food, I assure you. But where does one get prime food anymore in restaurants? Where, Chris?"

Ramsey gave the order and turned back to Chris.

"And now let's get to the matter at hand, as they say. What information do you wish from me?"

Chris hesitated.

"Come, Chris."

He had a pleasant smile. He was a tall man, just over six feet, with a supple, straight figure. His dark hair was just beginning to gray.

His voice was soft and modulated.

A man always in control of things and of himself, Chris thought. And he remembered his mother saying that of George Ramsey. And then he remembered the sad, dark look that would veil her eyes whenever she spoke of the man.

He never questioned her on that.

She never said a word.

"My Aunt Rhoda said you might not want to give

me the information. She said you once refused it to her."

"If I did, whatever it was, I had a good reason. And if I have a good reason, I will not give it to you either."

"Uh-huh."

The wine steward brought the bottle of wine to the table, poured a bit into Ramsey's glass, and waited. Ramsey took the glass gracefully and reached over and handed it to Chris.

"You judge it."

Chris took a sip of wine, while Ramsey watched him carefully, with a smile in his reflective brown eyes.

"Savor it."

"I am."

"Well?"

"It will do," Chris said.

Ramsey nodded to the steward to pour the wine.

"You want to find out about your inheritance, is that it, Chris?"

"Yes."

Ramsey waited till the steward left and then he began to speak.

"Any special reason?"

"No. Just curious."

Ramsey quietly studied him.

"Just curious. Your mother left a considerable fortune. It goes into quite a few million dollars. She left a part to your father and the bulk to you."

Chris waited.

"Your father got his and invested it all into a football team."

"And when will I get mine?"

Ramsey drank some wine and then set his glass down. Chris noted that he had long, delicate and supple fingers.

He had heard that Ramsey had been a squash

champion. A fine horseman. And an air force colonel during the Korean War.

As a combat pilot he had twenty-two kills to his record.

He has steel in him, Jamie would have said admiringly.

"When will you be eighteen?"

"In two weeks."

"What day of the week? I could have this looked up. But you tell me."

"Friday, the twelfth."

"Not Friday the thirteenth?"

"No. It falls on the twelfth this year."

Ramsey laughed, a quiet, low laugh.

"Friday is your lucky day. You will get your fortune then, Christopher Gordon, connoisseur of wines and good food." He laughed again. "But you won't get it. Not a nickel of it."

"What do you mean?"

"Under the terms of the will I am to oversee your inheritance until you are twenty-five years of age. So you have to come to me for every penny you might want."

"That's how Mother set it up?"

Ramsey nodded gravely.

"Yes. That's exactly how Marian Bentley wanted it. And that's exactly how it is going to be."

Chris buttered a small roll and then set the knife down.

"And if I die before my eighteenth birthday?"

Ramsey gazed quietly across the table and appraised Chris.

Nothing seems to faze you, Chris thought. You take everything in stride.

"Why do you ask that?"

"Just curious. Death is in the air these days. We're living in an atomic world."

"We are."

"Do you think mankind will make it? Or will we blow ourselves off the planet?"

"The money goes to your father," Ramsey said.

"Jamie?"

"Jamie Gordon."

They silently ate their food and then Chris spoke again.

"And if I die between the ages of eighteen and twenty-five?"

"Chris, what is this about dying?"

"The young think a lot about it these days, Mr. Ramsey."

Ransey's eyes darkened. His face became grave.

"Yes. I believe they do. But I'm sure you'll live to a comfortable old age."

"You haven't told me."

The steward came over and filled Ramsey's glass. When he turned to fill Chris's glass, Chris waved him away.

"You did that like the patrician that you are," Ramsey murmured.

"Patrician?"

"You dismissed him. With such grace and decision. The Bentley blood is quite strong in you. You're a young prince."

And Chris thought of Hamlet. He, too, was a prince. A young agonized prince whose destiny was a bloody death.

Ramsey sipped his wine and then said:

"Are you sure you'll have no more wine, Chris?"

"No. One glass is enough for me."

Ramsey smiled at him approvingly.

"You're not your father's son, are you?"

And Chris wondered how the man knew of Jamie's drinking. Away from home, Jamie always controlled his drinking and never once got himself into a scrape.

"You haven't told me," Chris said again.

"I haven't. Your entire inheritance becomes a bequest to the Metropolitan Museum of Art. Your Aunt Rhoda persuaded your mother to do that."

"So Jamie will get nothing?"

Ramsey gave Chris a piercing look.

"Nothing," he said.

Chris sat there, silent.

"Your steak," Ramsey said quietly. "It's getting cold."

"Yes."

But he did not pick up his knife. For the thought had come to him and he could not drive it away and it terrified him that he should even think such a thought...

That Jamie has only two weeks to get at the money. After that he is frozen out.

"Tell me," Chris said.

"Yes?"

"Did you like my father?"

Ramsey didn't answer.

"Do you like my father?"

Ramsey set his fork slowly and deliberately down onto the plate.

"I never liked your father. Nor do I like him now."

"My mother?"

"Why are you asking these questions?"

Chris shook his head.

"I don't know why. They just seem to come from within me."

"From within," Ramsey said.

A pale sadness seemed to come over his face. And for some reason, Chris felt himself being drawn close to the man.

Close and warm.

"Your mother," he murmured softly. "I was in love with Marian. And I had every reason to believe that she loved me. Every reason."

"What happened?"

"Jamie Gordon came along."

"Ah," Chris sighed out low.

I could have been your son, Chris thought, looking at the man. I would have liked being your son.

Ramsey lifted his glass and drank some wine and Chris thought that his hand shook ever so slightly.

Ramsey spoke again.

"In all justice I should not have told you this," he said. "It's unfair to Jamie Gordon. It should not matter to you in the least whether I like him or not. Or whether I was in love with your mother. Or still am."

"Still?"

"I have never married."

"You loved her that much?"

Ramsey looked steadily at him.

"Yes, Chris," he said in a low and even voice. "It is possible to love totally and forever. I have found it so."

And then he added gently:

"You may also find it so. But I hope you don't."

"Why?"

"Because it is a joy. And it is a torture."

And then the man spoke no longer. They ate in silence.

It was when the waiter was hovering behind them, waiting for them to call him over and order dessert, that Chris asked the question.

"How are his investments doing?"

"Whose?"

"My father's."

"I've no idea, Chris."

"I feel that you do. I wish you would tell me."

"Why? Curious again?"

"Yes."

Ramsey seemed to hesitate and then came to a decision.

"Your father is doing very badly these days. His team has been steadily losing money. There is a Chicago syndicate that wants to buy out Jamie Gordon and his partners."

"And?"

"The partners will gladly sell. But Jamie refuses to let go. If he can raise five million dollars he can hold them off. But he must do that quickly."

"They're crowding him?"

"To the wall, Chris. He has already been to see me to ask for help."

"He's that desperate?"

"I turned him down," Ramsey said coldly.

"He wanted some of the money that will come to me? A loan?"

"Yes."

"Football is his life," Chris said. "Without it he's a lost man."

He felt his heart go out to Jamie.

"I will not let him have a cent of your money. It was left in my trust."

"It's his life," Chris said again.

"I'm sorry about that."

"Without football he's a dead man."

"Dead?"

"It's as if somebody put a gun to his head."

"Oh. I thought you meant something else."

"What do you mean?"

"I thought you were talking literally."

Chris stared at the man.

"The syndicate has some pretty vicious people in it, Chris. They generally get what they want. One way or another. But I don't see them doing anything violent to a Jamie Gordon. He's still too much of a national celebrity."

"And he needs five million dollars to hold them off?"

"Nobody is going to give him that money, Chris. Not in today's world."

And Chris thought, Jamie forced to the wall would do anything to save his life.

Anything?

The waiter came over to them.

"What do you wish for dessert, Chris?"

Chris shook his head desolately.

"Nothing, Mr. Ramsey. I think I've had enough."

8

He was sitting on the terrace in the early morning, sipping his coffee and gazing out past the green leafy trees and down to the lake that glimmered in the misty sunshine, when he heard Ellen come over and sit down at the table.

"Chris?"

"Yes?"

"Do you mind if I sit a little while with you?"

"Not at all."

He was glad that she had come onto the terrace and he smiled at her. She had a haggard look about her and he felt that she had not slept the night.

"Did you have your breakfast?"

"Yes, Chris. I had it brought up to my room."

"Want some coffee?"

"No."

"Where's Jamie?" he asked casually.

"I don't know. He didn't come back last night. He's in the city."

"Oh?"

"Seeing some people."

Chris nodded and was silent.

"You staying home today?" she asked.

"No, Ellen. I'm taking a drive out to Seaside."

"Seaside? Where is that?"

"A little fishing village out on Long Island."

"What's there?"

"Oh, my mother used to go there in summertime. I thought I'd take a look at it again."

And he wondered why he said *again*. He had never been to Seaside in all his life.

"Want to take me along?"

"You?"

"I'd like to get away from here for the day. Be a little vacation for me. I'll be no trouble to you."

He looked at her, saw the plea in her eyes, and then he shook his head.

"No, Ellen. I want to do this one alone."

He saw that he had hurt her.

"You wouldn't understand even if I tried to explain it to you. It's too hard, Ellen," he said.

"It's okay with me, Chris."

A breeze rustled the leaves and the strands of her soft brown hair. He gazed at her sadness, so deep in her large, brown eyes.

I should trust her, he said to himself. I've always trusted her. From the first minute I saw her. I should take the envelope out of my pocket and show her the letter and tell her why I'm going to Seaside today.

Then he heard her voice.

"How's Lisa?"

"Lisa? She's all right."

"And the play?"

"Coming along."

"You're getting tickets for Jamie and me for opening night?"

"Yes, Ellen."

"Do you think it will be hard for me to understand a play like *Hamlet?*"

"No, Ellen," he said gently. "You'll get it better than anybody else in the audience. Believe me."

He still gazed at her and he thought of Rhoda's contemptuous words, "A waitress." He felt a hot pang of guilt go through him. He should have said to Rhoda,

Ellen has more gentleness and grace and true culture than you and all your society intellectuals will ever have.

Ever, Rhoda.

"Chris."

"Yes?"

"Jamie's a good father. He loves you."

"And?" Chris asked coldly.

She leaned forward and placed her hand on his arm. He felt a quiver of warmth run through him.

"Chris, why do you challenge him so much?"

"Do I?"

"You torture him."

"So?"

"Chris, please."

"Okay," he said grimly.

He looked away from her and down to the glimmer of water and he thought of his dead mother.

"He's a good man. You know that."

Is he, Ellen?

"He has his ways about him. But he's a good man."

He thought of his mother and saw again the blood dripping from her delicate hand. He felt his own hand tense and then slowly, slowly relax again.

Her voice came to him as from a distance.

"I sit here and sometimes I shiver," she said.

"Why, Ellen?"

She looked fully at him.

"Because I don't know what's going to happen here."

"What do you mean?"

She shook her head desperately and he saw tears in her eyes.

"I just don't know, Chris. I'm so afraid."

"Afraid of what, Ellen?"

But she got up and left him sitting there alone.

9

She was murdered.

I cannot reveal myself to you, for then, I, too, will be in danger of death. Just as you are now. For the murderer still lives.

He thought of these words as he drove on his way to Seaside. And he said to himself, All the odds are stacked against me. But I must take every chance I see. Maybe I'll get lucky. Maybe I'll find out who sent the letter.

And then I'll say:

Tell me. Who is the murderer?

Please.

You say you fear for your life. I do now for mine.

Tell me.

We both can do something about it.

Tell me.

Who killed my mother?

He drove along the narrow macadam road that followed the weaving coastline. The waters of the Sound sparkled and danced in the noon sun. It was a warm and golden day. Soon glorious summer would come.

Golden, golden summer.

But within him all the time was a chill, the bitter

chill of a dark winter's day. And it stayed within him as he came onto the little main street of the small, sleepy fishing village called Seaside.

So this is where you used to come, Mother, he thought to himself as he got out of the car and looked about him.

Long before you met Jamie.

Did you come here with George Ramsey?

Did you find peace and isolation and love with him?

Tell me, Mother, why do I know so little about you?

Why?

Why did you close off part of your life from me?

"Post office? It's just down the block. Only open a few hours a day."

"Is it open now?"

"Hard to say."

"Thanks," Chris said.

"Just walk east and stay east. You can't miss it."

"I won't."

"Where are you from?"

"Palance."

"Where's that?"

"Oh, a small town in Westchester."

"Small? Nothing's smaller than Seaside. So remember again, keep your eyes peeled and you won't miss it."

"Thanks again."

Chris smiled and began walking in the direction of the post office but something told him to turn around. And there was the man gazing quietly and coldly at him. The man who had been so genial in giving him directions.

He stood there, a dark figure against the high sun.

10

It was a little store with the words POST OFFICE on its window. The letter E was fading into obscurity. Chris went inside and there was nobody about. He walked to the open counter and stood waiting. There was a sheaf of government wanted posters hanging from a nail. He thumbed through it idly while waiting. He stopped at one which had in large letters WANTED FOR MURDER and he felt his heart begin to race.

The very word sets me off, he thought to himself.

He put the sheaf of posters back on the nail and breathed out low. Finally, an elderly woman, bustling and bright, came from the back room and over to the counter.

"Can I help you, young man?"

"I'm looking for the clerk."

"I'm the clerk."

He took out the envelope and showed it to her.

"Could you possibly remember this letter?"

The woman put on her glasses and studied the postmark. She nodded and smiled at Chris.

"This was mailed from here on Monday."

She took off her glasses and then put them slowly away into a pocket of her dress.

"Can I ask you a few questions about it?"

"Are you Christopher Gordon?"

"Yes."

"Any identification?"

Chris took out his driver's license and the woman went to her pocket and slowly took out her glasses and put them on again.

She nodded.

"You're him. Now what do you want to know?"

"Is it possible for you to remember who mailed this letter to me?"

She shook her head.

"Couldn't tell you, young man."

"Why not?"

"I wasn't here on Monday."

"Oh," Chris said.

"That would be Ed Foley."

"Any chance of my seeing him?"

"You have a car?"

"Yes."

"Well, drive south a mile and a half and you'll come across a dirt road that leads right to the water's edge. Ed's is the first house you come to."

"South a mile and a half. I got it."

"He should be sitting on his porch looking out at the boats and smoking his pipe."

"Thanks," Chris said.

"Wish you luck."

"I sure need it."

The woman looked gently and sympathetically at him.

"That letter must be very important to you."

"It is."

"Must be a matter of life and death to you."

He paled.

"What?"

She laughed, a low hearty laugh.

"Oh. I must have startled you by saying that."

"Yes. You did."

She laughed again.

"It's just an expression that we use around here for something important. Life and death. Doesn't mean anything."

"I guess it doesn't," Chris murmured.

The woman smiled at him, a broad motherly smile, and went back into the inner room again. Chris walked out into the brilliant sunshine.

He slowly, thoughtfully, returned to his car, got into it, and then drove slowly down the main street and past the tiny post office. The woman was standing on the sidewalk and as he passed her he waved to her but she gave no sign of recognition.

She gazed fully at him as he drove slowly past her and there was a wintry look in her gray eyes.

Cold and forbidding.

He felt his heart begin to race again.

11

He was sitting on the porch, smoking an old pipe, and gazing out at the reach of blue water. Chris walked up the three wooden steps that creaked and then he stopped. The man slowly turned his face to him.

"Well?"

"Mr. Foley? Ed Foley?"

"That's me."

He was a lean old man with a tanned, leathery, and seamed face and silver-gray hair. His eyes were blue and piercing. He had long arms and long legs and Chris figured that even at his age the man must stand straight as a rod, stand well over six feet.

Maybe even six three.

Just two inches short of Jamie.

Foley motioned to a chair near him.

"Take a seat."

Chris came over and sat down. There was a sound of a gull, a sharp cry, and then he saw it, far out over the water, a silvery shape, and he watched its sudden swoop and descent into the water and he heard the man's voice cut in.

"What do you want with me?"

Chris turned back to the man.

"I was told at the post office that you were on duty this past Monday."

"That's true."

"I wonder if you can help me out, Mr. Foley."

The man's piercing eyes were set upon Chris. Like two points of blue.

"How?"

Chris took out the envelope and handed it over.

"Could you possibly remember this letter? It came to me with no name or return address on it."

"You're Christopher Gordon?"

"Yes. I can show you my driver's license."

The man waved his big lean hand.

"No need to. I believe you."

He sat a while looking straight ahead of him. The envelope lay white in his lap. Chris sat near him waiting. Far out he could see the sails of boats flashing in the sunlight. And then at the very hairline of the horizon he made out the sharp black form of a freighter and then the dashes of black smoke curling up, up, until they forever lost themselves in the dazzling sky.

"Yes," the man said. "I remember the letter."

Chris turned abruptly away from the horizon and back to the man. He felt a trembling in his hands.

"You do?"

"Uh-huh. Have good reason to."

He paused and didn't speak. Then he picked up the envelope and silently handed it back to Chris.

Chris almost dropped it to the floor.

"Why, Mr. Foley?"

Foley lit his pipe and then blew out the flame of the wooden match. He then leaned forward and tossed the burned stick into his garden.

"Carbon is good for the flowers," he said wryly.

Chris waited.

"Why?" Foley suddenly said. "Because the lady who bought the stamps for it gave me a ten-dollar tip to make sure it got on its way properly."

"Lady?"

"Uh-huh. Now I'm not supposed to take a tip. But who does what he's supposed to do today? Especially when he's old and can use the money. You tell me."

"You remember the lady?"

Foley nodded vigorously.

"Of course I do. I told her to send it special delivery or register it. But she would have none of that. Yes, I remember her well."

"Can you describe her to me?"

"Sure. She drove up in one of those big new Mercedes cars. How much does a car like that cost these days? You know?"

"Silver-gray car?"

"That's right. Very pretty woman. But not young. Not old. How much would you say? It kind of piques me."

"About fifty thousand," Chris said.

The man's eyes widened.

"Fifty thousand."

"Copper hair. Blue eyes?"

"That's the woman."

"Rhoda Bentley," Chris murmured low.

"She gave me no name. Just the ten dollars."

"And then she drove off?"

"In a cloud of dust, as they say. Just sped right out of Seaside like the State Police was after her."

Chris looked out to the horizon. The black freighter was dipping out of sight. He kept looking till he could see it no more; only the white sails and the dazzling sunlight.

He slowly got to his feet and took a five-dollar bill out of his wallet. The old man waved the money away.

"I've been paid already," he said bluntly.

"Thank you, Mr. Foley," Chris said.

"Hope I've been of some use to you."

"You have."

"Fifty thousand."

"She has another one. A Rolls Royce," Chris said.

"And that one?"

"Over seventy-five thousand."

"The rich sure have money these days. Don't they?"

"They always had," Chris said.

He walked down the steps and then got into his car. The old man sat there on the porch watching Chris and he did not stir from his seat until he saw Chris drive away and out of sight.

He sighed out low.

Then he got up and went inside his small, neat house. The hall was cool and shadowy. He came to the telephone standing on a little oak table. He picked the receiver up and methodically dialed a long-distance number.

All about him the house was quiet and still. He looked through the open window and down at the placid stretch of green grass and he smiled, a sad, bitter smile. Ever since his wife died, his life had become quiet and still.

Like the quiet and stillness of death, he thought.

He heard the voice on the other end of the phone and then he began to speak.

"Ed Foley talking...He was just here...I told him exactly what you wanted me to...That you had a Mercedes and that you have blue eyes and copper hair and that..."

He nodded and then continued.

"Yes, just the opposite of what you really are ...Took it all in...Thanks...You gave me a fifty. And now you owe me another fifty...Fine, I'll be waiting for it."

He put down the phone and stood there, his figure straight as a rod. His eyes were a cold blue, impassive.

"A hundred dollars to play a joke on somebody," he said to himself in a low voice. "That's an awful lot of money. But some people have it to burn."

The old man shook his head and then went out

onto the porch and sat down again. He picked up his pipe.

"Maybe it's not a joke," he muttered.

He lit his pipe and then watched the flame die and the matchstick blacken.

"I guess I'm too old and alone to care," he said aloud.

Then he threw the matchstick into the garden and settled back into his chair. Out on the water the white sails flashed in the sun.

The horizon was blue and endless.

Soon he closed his eyes and slept.

12

"Rhoda Bentley. I must speak to her at once."

"Miss Bentley is not here now."

It was one of her maids.

"Well, where is she? This is her nephew, Chris."

"She's gone to the Coast, Mr. Gordon."

His hand tightened about the phone.

"What?"

"It's about a painting she wants to buy."

"Where on the Coast?"

"I don't know. When your aunt doesn't want to be disturbed she never leaves a forwarding address or a phone number. I believe you know that, Mr. Gordon."

"Yes. I know that," Chris said sullenly.

"Should she call in, I'll tell her you must speak to her."

She won't call in, Chris thought bitterly.

"How long will she be away?"

"At least a week."

I could be dead in a week, he thought. Then he shouted into the phone.

"Damn it, is this Margaret?"

"Yes, Mr. Gordon."

"Well, for God's sake, Margaret, you must help me."

"I don't know what to say to you, Mr. Gordon."

"Think. Try to think. Give me a clue."

"All I know is what I've told you. One of the galleries called her and told her of a painting she long wanted to acquire. That it was now for sale on the Coast and that she'd better get out there before another buyer beats her to it. That's all she told me."

...long wanted to acquire...

Margaret was beginning to speak like Rhoda. Why shouldn't she? Look at all the years she's been with her.

"That's all?" he asked.

"Yes."

When I was a little child, Margaret, you picked me up and held me in your arms. I remember it so well. I was crying and you comforted me.

And now you'll let me die.

"That's all I know, Mr. Gordon."

There was a desperate note to her voice. As if she knew his predicament and wanted to help him. But didn't know how.

Chris stood there looking through the glass walls of the phone booth, out at the stream of shining cars going by him on the highway. One after another. Endlessly.

All the drivers sealed off, one from the other.

All in their own tight little worlds.

If I were to open the doors of this booth and run out onto the road, my hands spread wide, run out and shout with a loud and piercing cry:

Help me. Help me.

I'm a dying man.

Help me!!!

Not one, not one damn one would stop.

They sit in metal coffins in a hopeless world.

An uncaring world.

A desolate one.

"Mr. Gordon."

He didn't speak.

73

"Mr. Gordon, are you still there?"

"Yes," he said.

"Is there anything else?"

"Nothing."

And then he said again:

"Nothing."

He hung up.

13

He was sleeping a restless, fearful sleep when suddenly he awoke and lay rigid and cold in his bed. Then he heard again the stealthy sounds that had wakened him. The sounds of light footsteps coming up the stairs to his room.

Slow and quiet.

One footstep softly after another.

One after another.

Like the flowing movement of a big cat.

He lay there, his eyes now wide open, the moonlight coming through the window in a swath of cold silver.

The sounds softly ended.

A great waiting silence.

And then he saw a massive black form blocking the doorway and its shadow angling against one of the walls of the room.

Like a dark spreading blot.

He gasped low as the figure glided softly into the room. Outside, the leaves of the silvery trees rustled and were silent.

The figure stood there in the black shadows of the room and then Chris could make out the large, gleaming eyes of his father.

He was about to cry out when he heard Jamie's voice.

"Chris?"

It was a whisper.

He didn't answer. He couldn't speak.

The big form moved closer to the bed, soundlessly.

"Chris, wake up. I've got to speak to you."

Chris slowly sat up in bed and gazed through the pale darkness at the massive figure of his father.

The glittering eyes held him.

"What do you want?"

"I can't sleep. I've got to talk to you."

"About what?"

Their voices were pitched low, shut off from the dark, silvery world about them. Their faces shimmered.

"Chris, I'm in the worst spot I ever was in in my whole life."

"And?"

"They're hemming me in. I've got nowhere to turn anymore. It's third and long, Chris. Third and long. I'll never make it."

"So?"

"Chris, Chris, you've got to help me. You can save me."

"How?"

His words were cold and tight and all the time he was staring into his father's large eyes.

"I need money. I need it bad. You can give it to me."

"I?"

"Speak to Ramsey and convince him to lend me the money."

"So that's it, Jamie."

"Chris, why are you so turned off? Why? Why can't you feel for me?"

Feel for you, Claudius?

You are a murderer, Claudius.

He heard his father's voice come to him.

"Just a loan. I'll pay it back. Every cent of it."

Chris could see drops of sweat gleaming on his father's massive forehead. He wondered if Jamie had been drinking.

Then he heard the low and intense voice.

"You'll get your money in a week and a half, Chris. You'll be eighteen then."

If I live, Claudius.

"I can wait that time. If Ramsey will promise that I will get it. If he can put it in writing. That will hold them off. Chris, there are a bunch of wolves waiting to tear me apart. Help me."

"Ramsey won't do it. You know that already."

"It's your money," Jamie said in a fierce voice. "Yours."

Yes, he has been drinking, Chris thought. *Drinking too much. It's burning in him, like a low fire.*

Who knows what he'll do when the fire suddenly shoots up to his brain.

Look at those eyes. Just look at those eyes.

The mad eyes of King Claudius, the murderer.

The very same eyes that Hamlet looked into with fear and dread.

"Sure it's my money, Jamie," he said. "But he controls it."

"Control?"

Jamie's big hand came up in a fist and the silvery moonlight flashed off it. Chris flinched backward.

"To hell with that. It's your money. To give me if you want to. And you want to, Chris. Don't you?"

Chris didn't speak.

Jamie moved closer, his huge figure blotting out the rest of the room.

"Damn it, it's a small part of what's waiting for you. You'll still have all those millions left. You couldn't spend that money in two lifetimes. What the hell is it to you, Chris? I'm your father."

He moved even closer and now he loomed over his son.

77

"Jamie," Chris whispered.

He trembled.

I fear you now, my father.

God only knows how I fear your savage strength.

I sit here pinned against the wall and nowhere to turn.

"I need the money and you have it, Chris. You have it."

"I have it," Chris said.

"Then make him give it to me."

"I can't make him do anything."

Jamie's eyes glittered wildly in the shadows. His voice became tight and harsh.

"Make him do it, Chris. I'm warning you."

"Warning me?"

A tremor went through Chris.

The fire is now in his mad brain, he thought. Christ, help me.

"Make him do it. Do you hear me? Or else..."

"Or else what, Jamie?"

"Make him."

And Chris, staring into the tense face that was so close to him, feeling the hot breath on him, now knew what his father was saying to him.

Your life is on the line, Chris. You make him do it or I'll have to wipe you out. Kill you before you become eighteen. Then the money will go to me.

Damn you, Chris, I'll get the money one way or another.

The same way I got it six years ago when your mother wouldn't give it to me.

It's on the line, Chris. My life or yours.

Well, what will it be?

"Well, Chris?"

"I'll speak to him," Chris said.

"Will you?"

"Yes."

"Will you?"

"I told you I will."

Jamie suddenly leaned forward and fiercely grabbed hold of Chris.

"You must do it."

"Let me go."

"You must!"

"Jamie!"

Chris desperately twisted out of the grip and moved back to the wall. Jamie stood there, breathing heavily, his body hunched forward, his hands out in front of him.

Chris tensed and waited for Jamie to go at him again.

"Chris."

The voice was low and bewildered. And suddenly the giant body went slack. Jamie stood there gazing through the shadows at his son.

The large black eyes stared at Chris as if seeing him for the first time.

"Chris..."

The voice trailed off into silence. The face was now that of a huge, penitent child.

"Chris...I...I didn't mean to grab you like that."

"I know, Jamie," Chris said grimly. "You didn't mean to. But you did."

"Be easy."

"Easy?"

And now a cold rage swept through him.

You didn't mean to. Just as you didn't mean to kill my mother.

"Forgive me, Chris. I'm not myself. I don't know what I'm doing these days. You're right, I drink too much. I've got to listen to you and cut it down. You're right, Chris. I've got to do it."

He looked at Chris, his eyes now filled with a tender anxiety.

"I tore your pajama top. Did I hurt you?"

"No."

"Did I?"

"I said no."

Jamie held out his hand forlornly to his son, but Chris would not take it.

"Shake and forgive?"

"Let it be, Jamie."

How did you kill her, Jamie? Damn you, tell me.

"I'm not myself," Jamie murmured.

His hand fell to his side hopelessly.

"Did I ever hit you, Chris? Did I? Did I?"

Chris didn't answer him.

"I love you, Chris. You know that."

"Yes, Jamie. I know."

I'll find out the truth. I will, King Claudius. And then you'd better watch out for yourself, my father.

For I am your son, too.

Remember that.

Remember that well.

"We're on the same team together, Chris. Aren't we?"

"Yes, Jamie."

"Teammates never really fight with each other. Do they?"

"No, Jamie," he said, as if speaking to a child.

"We're on the same team."

"Yes."

"Third and long. But together we'll make it. Right, Chris?"

"Right, Jamie."

Your son, Jamie. Remember that. For I can be just as cruel as you are. You put that black streak into me when you became my father.

Always remember that.

"Chris."

"Well?"

"Chris, don't look at me that way. Please don't."

"What way?" Chris asked savagely.

But Jamie didn't answer.

Chris watched the big man turn and go silently out of the room. He sat there listening to the footsteps going down the stairs.

One after another.

Like the flowing movement of a big cat.

Silence slowly spread over the staircase.

And now he was alone in the darkness and the terror.

14

He was sitting on the stone bench looking out over the lake, watching the morning mists begin to rise and thin away, when he heard her approach. At first, he thought it was Ellen, but then he turned and saw the slender figure of Lisa.

He felt his heart quicken as he rose. He realized how far he had drifted away from her.

I'll lose her before this is over, he said to himself. One way or another I'll lose her.

As I may lose my life.

"Hello, Lisa."

She smiled, a sad smile, and sat down on the bench.

"Ellen said you'd be down here."

"Oh."

"Glad to see me?"

"Uh-huh."

They sat silently side by side and then the sun suddenly broke through and he saw the light glint off her hair.

He bent forward and gently kissed her hair.

"That was nice, Chris."

"You're nice," he said.

There was always something so delightful and fragrant about her, he thought. If I were older and things were different, I would ask her to marry me.

I really mean that.

But I'm not older.

And things will not be different.

And so I shall lose her.

"Am I, Chris?"

"Yes."

They kissed and then he took her warm, trembling hand in his and they were silent again. Out on the lake a golden perch broke the water, sparkled in the sun, and then slid back in again, and the lake was broad and calm as before.

He thought of the time Jamie had the lake stocked and how he used to go fishing with him almost every morning.

In the good and golden times.

When he was young and trusting and innocent.

"I think Ellen likes you very much," Lisa said.

"Ellen?"

"Yes."

He wondered what was coming next.

"I think she's in love with you."

"What?"

"I don't think she's in love with your father."

He gazed out at the lake and didn't say anything.

"I don't think she ever was, Chris."

He turned back to her.

"And you're basing this on?"

"My woman's intuition."

"Oh," he said.

"You don't think much of a woman's intuition, do you?"

"Didn't say a thing."

"But it's all there. In your eyes."

"Is it?"

"Right."

She brushed her hair back with a sweep of her hand and then spoke again.

"I disturb you with what I said?"

"Just made me think about things. That's all."

"She's older than you. But older people are falling in love with younger people and younger people with older and everything's all mixed up and absurd these days. So there you have it."

She was now smiling broadly at him. But deep, deep in her eyes the sadness still lay there.

He saw it and it touched him to his heart.

"You've been putting me on, haven't you?" he said softly.

She shook her head and her hair swung and flashed in the sun. He wanted to lean over and kiss her again but he didn't.

Just sat there, feeling her sadness in his heart.

"No. Just in a kind of speaking-the-truth mood."

"And that's why you came down here?"

"That's why."

She wasn't smiling anymore.

"Tell me," he said. "While you're in this mood. What do you really think of my father?"

"Jamie?"

"Jamie."

He waited.

"I guess I think of him in the same way most women do."

"And what is that?"

"He's a huge, very handsome, gentle and lovable man."

"You're not putting me on?"

"No, Chris."

And he could see that she was speaking the truth.

"He's as handsome as you are, Chris, in his way. And he's as gentle as you are."

"Gentle? You feel Jamie is a gentle person?"

"Don't you?"

"Yes," he said.

But within him, he said, How can I ever tell you the truth about him, Lisa? How?

Her voice was soft.

84

"Chris, he's nothing but a big child that asks for mothering. And a lot of women like to mother."

"I guess they do," he murmured.

He thought of George Ramsey and of how he had had to go into the city to plead with him today. Please give gentle Jamie the money he wants.

Please, or gentle Jamie will kill me.

"You don't see him as a violent person," he heard himself say.

"On the football field. And that's where it is right to be violent. To let it all out. That's why he's so kind and lovable off the field."

He looked out over the small lake and he thought of his mother sitting on the bench with him, as Lisa was sitting now.

"You think my mother saw him the same way as you do?"

"Positive. She was very happy with him."

"Happy? You were too young to know that."

"I was twelve when she died. Your age. A girl matures quicker than a fellow. I was not too young. She loved him, Chris, and they were very happy together."

"And he loved her," Chris said, and he could barely control his bitterness.

"With all his heart. It was a true love match. Don't you feel the same way?"

"Yes," he said.

"But you don't," she said.

Now she was looking fully at him, her eyes clear and cold.

"I didn't say that, Lisa."

"You don't have to."

He turned away from her and was silent. Little waves rippled in the sun. The leaves of trees floated noiselessly. The sky above was blue and cloudless.

All was so peaceful, he thought bitterly.

So very peaceful.

God's in his heaven and all's right with the world.

Except with me.

With me.

He felt her rise from her seat and still he didn't turn.

"Chris," she said.

"Yes?"

"What's going on between you and Jamie?"

"Me and Jamie?"

"And Ellen."

He rose and faced her.

"Nothing," he said.

"We know each other a long time, Chris."

And I've held you in my arms, Lisa. Don't bring that up. Please. Not now.

"I really came down here to speak of us. We're through with each other, aren't we, Chris?"

"Lisa," he said hoarsely.

"Something has pulled you away from me. And it's all over, isn't it?"

"No."

Her eyes flashed.

"Don't lie to me, Chris. You were never a liar."

"I'm not."

She shook her head fiercely.

"I'll still do the play with you. Because others are involved. But with us it's over. If you haven't the guts to say it to me, I have to say it to you."

"Lisa..."

He wanted to say so much more but his voice failed him.

"Good-bye, Chris. It was great while it lasted. I'm thankful for that."

She turned and walked away from him.

"Lisa," he called.

But she did not pause or stop and he was left standing alone with nothing but her lingering fragrance.

And soon even that faded away.

15

"Mr. Ramsey will be with you in a few minutes. He's at a board meeting," the secretary said. "He asked me to have you wait in his private office."

"Fine," Chris said.

"Please make yourself comfortable."

"Sure."

"Mr. Ramsey doesn't smoke."

"I don't either."

The secretary went out, closing the door behind her. The room was high and silent. Chris looked about him at the paneled walls, the curtained windows, and then at the richly upholstered chairs. Ramsey's office was on the fortieth floor of a new skyscraper just off Wall Street. Through one of the windows Chris could see the shining Twin Towers of the World Trade Center.

He sits here at the very heart of things, Chris thought. Calm and sure of himself. Always makes the right moves.

Always quiet and poised.

Mr. Ramsey doesn't smoke. He sets the rules and you follow them. You had better follow them. There is no other way with him.

Always in control. Of others and of himself.

How different he is from Jamie.

There was a large mahogany desk placed just off the center of the room and on it was a silver framed photograph, its back to Chris.

He sat there staring at it.

The secretary opened the door again and went to the desk and placed some documents on it, smiled warmly at Chris, and then went out again, closing the door quietly.

The silence continued.

Chris got up from his seat and went over to the desk and then around it till he faced the photograph.

He stood still.

It was a picture of his mother. His young mother. Her face was warm and radiant. Her eyes glowing.

He bent over and read the inscription.

George, I shall always love you, Marian.

"Always," he murmured softly.

Was always a short time with you, Mother? Until Jamie came along? Or was it forever?

Did you never stop loving George Ramsey?

Chris felt a gentle hand on his shoulder.

"She was a beautiful woman. Wasn't she, Chris?"

"Yes," Chris said.

"An unforgettable woman. We both know that, don't we, Chris?"

"Yes."

Ramsey patted Chris and then pointed to a chair. He sat down at his desk, glanced at the documents there for an instant, and then pressed a button. The door opened and his secretary appeared.

"I don't want to be disturbed until Mr. Gordon leaves."

"Yes, Mr. Ramsey."

The door closed and Ramsey turned to Chris.

"You said it was urgent."

"That's right."

"Tell me about it."

"It has to do with my father."

"I thought so," Ramsey said quietly.

"He desperately needs money."

"And he's come to you."

"Yes."

"Begged you to come to me and plead his case for him."

"Begged?"

"Didn't he?"

Ramsey's eyes were quietly probing into Chris.

"Yes," Chris murmured. "Begged."

How much of the truth do you know of Jamie? Chris wondered.

"Chris, I told you he was here already."

"I know that."

"And you also know that I turned him down. Coldly. Flatly."

The man's voice was crisp.

"Yes."

"Then why are you here?"

"Because you can't turn him down again," Chris said.

Ramsey gazed at Chris, a reflective look in his eyes.

"Why can't I?"

Because he'll kill me if I don't get the money, Chris wanted to shout at him.

"He's against the wall."

"He is."

"I have so much coming to me. It's in the millions. Why in the world can't I...Why?...Why..."

His voice trailed out into silence.

Ramsey finally spoke.

"Yes. You have a tremendous fortune coming to you. And you're going to get every penny of it, while I'm in control. That's how Marian wanted it, Chris."

Chris leaned forward to the man.

"He's my father. Can't I help my own father?"

Ramsey shook his head.

"Not if he's going to lose four or five million dollars of your money."

"How do you know that he'll lose it?"

Ramsey sighed gently.

"It's my profession to know these things, Chris. I am an authority in these matters. And I am speaking modestly."

"I want to help him," Chris said.

"I know you do and I appreciate your deep concern. But I must say that because I care so much for you and your..."

"No," Chris suddenly cut in. "You don't care for me. You don't. You want to see me...to see me..."

He stopped speaking.

"To see what, Chris? You were about to say something."

Chris was silent.

"Please tell me."

Ramsey's eyes were boring into Chris, as if trying to get to the core of his secret.

"It's nothing."

"I'm sure it is not."

"You wouldn't believe me even if I told you."

"Try me."

"No."

"Chris, many people confide in me. To their great advantage. Why can't you?"

Chris looked across the desk and into the face of George Ramsey. My mother loved this man, he thought to himself. Can I say to him, Jamie wants to kill me. Would he believe it? Christ in heaven, would anybody in this world believe that my own father would kill his own son? His only son?

All for that goddamned money?

"Chris."

I'm beginning to hate that money with all my soul.

"It was nothing," Chris said harshly.

"But it wasn't."

"Damn it, let it alone."

"If you want it that way," Ramsey said quietly and leaned back in his chair.

"Yes."

My mother put a curse on me when she left me that money. Why in the hell didn't she give it all to Jamie and let him do with it whatever the hell he wanted?

Why?

I've lost Lisa. And I'll lose my life before this is over.

He heard himself speak again and he didn't recognize his voice.

"I'm asking you for the last time. Give him the money. For my sake."

"It is for your sake that I can't give him the money."

Chris sprang up from his chair, his face taut, his eyes wild.

"My sake?" he shouted. "No. No. You don't give a damn about me."

"Chris."

"You don't. You're a liar."

Ramsey flinched backward as if Chris had slapped him. He rose, tall and pale. But he did not speak.

"A liar," Chris shouted again.

"You could have been my son," Ramsey said in a low and even voice. "By all rights you should have been my son. I care more for you than for anybody on this living earth."

"You lie. All you can think about is how to destroy Jamie for what he did to you. Isn't that the truth? Isn't it?"

"It is not that at all. And you know it."

Chris waved his hand at him bitterly.

"I was a fool to come here."

"Chris, sit down and calm yourself. And then let's talk."

"No."

"Please, Chris."

"A fool," Chris shouted.

Then he turned and walked out of the room.

George Ramsey slowly went back to his desk and

slowly sat down. Finally, he pressed a button and soon the door opened and his secretary stood on the threshold of the large room.

"I want to speak to Rhoda Bentley. Locate her if it takes you the entire day. Drop everything else and find her."

"Yes, Mr. Ramsey."

The door closed and Ramsey sat there silently, not moving. Then he turned and gazed at the photograph and a haunted look came over his face.

"Why, Marian?" he murmured softly. "Why did you do it?"

16

When he came back from the city, he went looking for Jamie and found him in the trophy room. Jamie was sitting in his big leather chair, a large cowboy hat on his head, and in his right hand he held one of his pearl-handled forty-fives. The other gun lay balanced on the arm of the chair.

The afternoon light came through the barred windows and glinted off the barrels of the guns.

Jamie cried out with joy the instant he saw Chris.

"Chris. My son. My only son."

It's happy time, Chris thought sardonically. Playtime for the big child. He's been drinking and it's put a good blurry feeling into him. Fogged him out. He's forgotten last night and he's forgotten why I went into the city.

He's forgotten.

For the moment.

"Hello, Chris," Ellen said softly.

"Hello, Ellen."

"Where've you been?"

"The city."

"Anything special?"

He shook his head.

"Nothing. Just went in to see a friend."

"Have a good time?"

"Uh-huh."

"Lisa go with you?"

"No," he said.

She was sitting in one of the easy chairs, a fashion magazine in her lap. She had looked up from it when he came into the room.

"Jamie's been waiting for you." She smiled.

But deep in her eyes he could see her anxiety and her fear.

"Sure have," Jamie shouted. "Hiyah, cowboy."

"Hiyah, cowboy," Chris said.

"Take a gun, pardner."

Jamie picked up the gun that was on the arm of the chair and tossed it across the room to Chris. Chris caught it deftly and sat down.

He's in his cowboy mood, Chris thought. He's back on the ranch with his daddy. And soon he'll have me play the game with him.

One of his all-time favorites.

God, how I used to like playing it with him.

And how I now despise and fear it.

"Let's practice some draws," Jamie said.

"No, Jamie."

"C'mon, give me a break. You always beat me. I feel lucky today."

"Some other time, Jamie."

"You're the only one in the entire country who ever could beat me. You've got to give me a break today, pardner."

"There'll be other days, Jamie. I'm not in the mood."

"Then get yourself in it, pardner."

"No."

Jamie chuckled and shook his head wonderingly.

"I never turned down my daddy when he wanted to play draw with me."

"Some other time."

"Never turned down my daddy. Know why?"

"Why?"

94

"Because I loved him. That's why."

"I'm sure you did," Chris said.

"And you love me, don't you, Chris?"

Chris looked across the room at the big, hearty, smiling face. The cowboy hat was pushed far back and beads of sweat showed on the massive forehead.

"Yes, Jamie," he said.

"Then play draw. I've got a mighty hunger for it, pardner."

"He doesn't want to, Jamie," Ellen said quietly.

Jamie turned slowly to her and the merry glint was gone from his eyes.

"Stay out of it, Ellen," he said.

They gazed at each other in silence and then she lowered her head.

"All right," she murmured.

He turned back to Chris and he began to laugh again, a low, pleased laugh.

"C'mon, Chris. C'mon, pardner."

Chris looked over at Ellen and she nodded hopelessly to him.

"I'm awaitin' your move," Jamie said.

And now Chris saw a plea in her eyes.

"Okay," he said wearily. "I'll play."

Jamie hit his knee with his big hand, chuckled and rose from his chair.

"Thanks, pardner. You sure do love your ole foolish daddy, don't you?"

"We'll check the guns," Chris said.

Jamie stared at him.

"I just took them out of the case, Chris."

"I know that."

"They're never loaded when they set there in the glass case, Chris. What do you think I am? A damn fool?"

Chris didn't answer him. He broke open his gun and flipped the cylinder. He found no bullets in the gun.

"Mine's okay."

"Of course it's okay."

"Check yours, Jamie," he said quietly.

"I told you that all the guns in the case are not loa..."

"Check it, or no game," Chris cut in grimly.

Chris gazed across the room at his father. He could see Ellen's face in the shaded background.

It had become tense and anxious. He thought she was about to cry out.

"Sure thing, Chris," Jamie said slowly.

He broke open the gun, flipped the cylinder and then nodded.

"Empty."

"Okay."

"You want to come over and examine it yourself?"

Chris shook his head.

"No."

"You want Ellen to examine it?"

"No."

"Satisfied?"

"Yes, Jamie."

"And you still love and trust your daddy?"

"Yes, Jamie."

"All the way?"

"All the way."

"Just like I always trusted my daddy?"

"Just like you always trusted your daddy."

"Good."

Jamie suddenly laughed and his hearty laughter filled the room. It was such a warm and good sound that it brought a smile to Ellen's face.

And even to Chris's lips.

Just a big overgrown kid, Chris thought. A kid. Am I wrong about him? Is Lisa right and am I so desperately wrong?

"Ready, pardner?"

"Ready."

Chris tucked the gun into the waistband of his

jeans. Then he watched Jamie tuck his into his waistband.

"Move back two steps," Jamie called.

"Right."

The two moved farther backward from each other. They stood ready, their shadows falling across the floor of the room.

"You speak to Ramsey?" Jamie suddenly asked.

"Yes."

"And?"

"No dice, Jamie."

The eyes became flinty and cold and then suddenly Jamie laughed and his huge body shook with his laughter.

Chris waited for him to stop.

"To hell with him," Jamie finally said. "I'll come up with it. One way or another. But I'll come up with it."

"Will you?"

"Yes."

They stood facing each other and now the room was entirely still.

"Draw."

Chris grabbed the gun from his waistband with a deft and sure motion and pointed it at Jamie. But Jamie's gun was already in his hand, aimed at his son's chest.

"Beat you this time."

"You did."

"The only time I ever beat you."

"Right."

"It is my lucky day."

Jamie's laugh again filled the room, merry and exultant.

"And now, pardner, I let you have it."

"Go ahead." Chris smiled.

And he never knew why he did it, but something within him told him to move and as he did, Jamie squeezed the trigger and there was a flash and a roar.

A bullet grazed past Chris's head and thudded into the wall behind him.

Then they heard Ellen's scream.

"Chris."

She screamed again and her very soul seemed to be in her voice.

"Chris."

He stood pale and trembling, staring at Jamie.

"Chris."

She ran past Jamie and came up to Chris and grabbed him to her.

"Are you all right?"

He didn't speak.

"Chris. Chris."

She held him close to her and began to sob. He stroked her hair and tried to comfort her but she continued to sob, her body shaking violently.

"I'm okay, Ellen," he said.

"No. No."

"Okay," he murmured softly.

Slowly she gained control of herself. But still she held him to her.

"You're all right?"

He nodded.

"Yes, Ellen. Yes."

The tears streamed down her face. Her body still trembled.

"You were almost killed."

"Almost," he said.

"You moved just in time."

He nodded.

"Yes."

"What made you move?" she asked and her voice had lowered to a whisper.

He shook his head.

"I don't know."

"You moved. Thank God, you moved."

And all the time Jamie stood there, looking down at the gun which had dropped from his limp hand to the floor.

"It was empty. I swear to you it was empty."

He said the word over and over again.

"Empty. Empty."

His voice was low and hushed as if he were talking to himself. The barred shadows fell across his huge body.

He stood there, hunched forward.

"Empty. Empty."

He stopped speaking.

Suddenly he slid down on both knees to the floor beside the gun and was silent as a statue.

A glazed look came into his large black eyes.

"Empty," Chris said in a loud, cutting voice.

Then Chris saw his father's face begin to twist up and soon Jamie was weeping silent tears.

And as Chris looked at the man a rage overwhelmed him.

"You drunken bastard," he shouted. "Get out of my life."

Then he went out of the room, leaving Jamie and Ellen alone with each other.

17

He didn't want to go to rehearsal that night but then he said to himself, I must go. It's the only way I'll keep myself sane. The only way I'll be able to think things through.

By keeping my mind off Jamie and that murder money that he hungers for so desperately.

And so for the first hour and a half he did quite well. He remembered all of his lines and he put himself completely into the role and felt a great sense of power and of release.

A feeling of utter peace came over him. And he wished that he would never have to leave the theater and go home.

When one of the scenes was over, he went off by himself and stood against one of the wings, smiling and thinking of the stirring words of the play.

The director, Mr. Caldwell, came over to him.

"You were quite good in that scene, Chris," he said.

"Thanks. I felt good. Sure of myself."

"Yes. I sensed that."

They were standing away from the others, talking quietly. Chris felt that Mr. Caldwell had come over to him with a definite purpose in mind.

He wondered what it was.

"I liked the way you turned to Laertes and paused a few beats before speaking. Seemed to look through him. A very good touch, Chris."

Chris smiled, pleased.

"It sort of came naturally," he said.

Caldwell nodded.

"First time you did it that way. Keep it in."

"I will, Mr. Caldwell."

Caldwell glanced about him with his alert, thoughtful eyes. He was a tall, slender man with graying hair.

He was one of the best-liked persons on the faculty.

"I believe we're going to have a fine production. One that we'll all be very proud of, Chris."

Chris nodded.

"Everybody seems to think that way, Mr. Caldwell."

Caldwell smiled.

"I'm very fortunate in my cast. It's an exceptionally good one this year."

"Yes."

"Lisa is a lovely Ophelia. Don't you think so?"

"She is."

And he felt that Caldwell was now studying him, trying to probe within. The rest of the cast had left the stage and now the two were completely alone.

The auditorium was dark and silent.

Only the stage was lit.

Chris waited for Caldwell to speak again.

"Chris."

"Yes?"

"In your scenes with Lisa. You seem to have become cold and distant with her. It was not so in the past rehearsals."

Chris was silent.

"Do you agree with me?"

"Maybe," Chris said reluctantly.

"What's causing it?"

Chris shrugged.

"Chris, I have no right to go into this. But I feel it affects the entire production. Has anything happened that...?"

He didn't go on.

"Everything's fine between us," Chris said.

"I understand that you were close friends."

"We still are."

Caldwell looked at him and then shook his head. And as he did that, the gesture and look reminded Chris for some reason of George Ramsey.

"Chris," he said gently. "I must be blunt with you. I've been worried about you lately."

"Worried?"

"That's right."

"Why?"

Caldwell hesitated and then went on.

"You seem to lose your concentration at times. As if you had some deep personal problems that were distracting you."

"Oh."

"I feel rather awkward in bringing this up."

"I understand."

He does remind me of George Ramsey, Chris thought. The way he's probing into me. Wherever I turn these days, I'm confronted with my destiny.

I'm being hemmed in, more and more.

He heard Caldwell's voice.

"It's just that there's so much at stake here. You're well aware of that, Chris."

"Yes."

Caldwell paused and then said gently:

"Are there any problems, Chris?"

Chris shook his head.

"None, Mr. Caldwell."

"I feel that there are. Won't you discuss them with me?"

"There are none at all," Chris said.

"You're sure now?"

"Yes."

And he thought to himself, You're a good and decent man. And we all like you so very much. I've always felt close to you. But there's nothing, nothing you can do for me. It's out of your world.

So completely out of your world, Mr. Caldwell.

It seems that nobody can help me.

Nobody.

Caldwell smiled tenderly at Chris and then patted him.

"All right then. I've tried."

"Thanks just the same. But everything's fine."

"If you say so."

"I do."

Caldwell sighed gently.

"Take a break. And then we'll do the nunnery scene. I think you and Lisa need a little more work on it."

"I thought we had it down fine," Chris said.

"Just a bit more work, Chris."

"Okay," Chris murmured.

And then he went outside into the night air and stood among the trees and stared up at the stars.

And thought.

If I hadn't moved, the bullet would have smashed into my head and killed me. Killed me instantly.

A clean, precise murder.

But it all would have been called a tragic accident.

Jamie would have stressed that we've played that game many times before. The winner of the draw always pointed the gun at the chest of the loser and squeezed the trigger. In triumph.

And nothing ever happened.

I remember saying to Jamie that one shouldn't point a gun at another person at any time. I said it when we first started playing the game, some years back. But Jamie laughed and said, Chris, I was brought up with guns. I'm the most careful fellow in the world with guns. Before a gun is put back into the glass case it is thoroughly examined by me. When we play the game, the guns are always taken out of the glass case. You and I are the only ones who have keys to the case. No chance in a million for a bullet to be in any of the guns.

And his eyes would light up like a child's.

Isn't it more fun when you finish the draw and you're a winner and then you have the joy of shooting down the other gunslinger like they always did in the West?

Isn't it?

That's how my daddy played the game with me. And that's how your daddy plays the game with you. And that's how when you're a daddy you'll play it with your son.

Right, Chris?

Chris breathed in sharply as if a knife had cut into him.

No chance in a million, he thought.

And yet this time there was a bullet in the gun. And I saw Jamie examine it. Or did he really?

Did he lie to me?

Yet he offered the gun to me to examine. And then to Ellen.

Was that a bluff?

Did he know I would refuse him?

The bullet was in the gun when he examined it. He had to see it when he spun the cylinder. But then again, he had been drinking too much and it could be possible that with his blurred mind and vision he missed it.

But even so, how did it get into the gun in the first place? Who else could have put it there but Jamie?

And so I'm back to my dear father.

To bloody Claudius.

A tragic accident happens in the trophy room. And Jamie Gordon inherits the full estate of his dead son, Christopher Gordon.

The lad is killed in a very tragic domestic accident. The father is grief-stricken. Inconsolable.

A goddamned lie.

He tried to kill me.

For that money. That blood money.

"Chris?"

Chris turned and saw Lisa come out of the lit building and walk toward him and into the shadowed darkness of the trees.

He felt himself tremble all over and he realized how much he needed her. He could not go on any longer without her.

He must tell her everything.

He must or he'd fall apart.

"Lisa."

"Mr. Caldwell wants us."

Her face was white and cold in the half-light. It made her only the more beautiful to him.

"Lisa," he said. "I must talk to you. Please."

He felt her fragrance and it filled him with a terrible yearning for her. Just to hold her close and forget everything.

To hold her close. Close.

"There's nothing to talk about, Chris."

"Please."

"It was all said."

He shook his head desperately.

"No. It wasn't."

"They're waiting for us."

"Lisa. I want to tell you everything."

"What do you mean?"

"I've been keeping back a terrible truth from you."

She stared silently at him.

"I want you to share it with me. To help me."

He held out his hands to her pleadingly.

"I need your help. I need you. Lisa. Lisa."

Her eyes softened, her lips trembled.

"All right, Chris," she said tenderly. "We'll talk later."

He drew her to him and kissed her.

"Lisa," he whispered.

"Chris."

She drew away but her eyes were glowing.

"Later. They're waiting, Chris."

"Okay."

He started back to the building with her, a feeling of peace descending upon him. He felt close to tears of relief.

But as they entered the building, she paused.

"There's a note on the bulletin board. For you."

A strange look seemed to come into her eyes.

"Okay. I'll pick it up on the way in."

"I'll go on ahead."

"Sure."

He watched her go into the stage area, the light catching her hair softly, and then he could see her no more.

Lisa.

He thought only of Lisa, Lisa, and of how much he yearned for her. He could never lose her again.

Never.

It would be too much to bear.

Lisa.

Then he saw the note on the bulletin board and he walked over to it. He saw the typewritten words on the white face of the envelope and he felt a chill go through him till he began to tremble.

> Christopher Gordon
> Gordon Estate
> Country Road
> Palance, New York

He pulled out the thumbtack and then took the envelope into his hand. He stood there for what seemed to him to be an eternity before he slowly opened the envelope and took out the typewritten note.

He read it.

Claudius knows that you know. Claudius, the murderer, knows. Hamlet, defend yourself.

He has made his decision.

It is his life.

Or yours.

Hamlet, make your decision.

Kill him.

Before he kills you.

Ophelia

Chris crumpled the note into his fist and stood there, breathing heavily, his face white with anger and fear.

"Ophelia," he said.

Then he jammed the note into his pocket and walked very slowly away from the bulletin board.

"Ophelia," he said again.

His voice sounded hollow and strange to him. The voice of a person who had split away from him.

When he came onto the stage, Caldwell was talking to Lisa about her lines. He stopped speaking and stared at Chris.

Then he came swiftly over to him.

"Chris, what is the matter?"

"What?"

"You look as if you've just seen a ghost."

"What?" Chris asked again.

Caldwell put his hand on Chris's shoulder.

"Are you all right?"

"There are no ghosts. Only murderers," Chris said.

He moved sharply away and the man's hand dropped to his side.

"Chris."

"I'm all right," Chris said.

Caldwell looked anxiously at him.

"Chris, I feel that you should..."

His voice trailed off into silence. In the background, Lisa stood there pale and trembling.

No one else was in the auditorium but these three.

The light fell across them, the naked light and the filtered darkness.

Their faces and bodies were shadowed and lit.

They stood on the empty stage, spaced apart from each other, like three characters in an ancient tragic play. They stood there, bare and alone.

"I'm all right," Chris said.

"Do you still want to do the scene?"

"Yes."

"We could forget it and do it tomorrow."

The voices were empty and had a slight echo.

"No."

"Maybe you should go on home and get yourself a..."

"Home?" Chris cut in bitterly. "I have no home."

Caldwell stared at him.

"Chris," he said gently.

"Let's do the scene and get it over with."

His voice echoed over the stage and then it faded away. The seats of the auditorium extended row upon row into a silent darkness.

"All right, Chris," Caldwell said quietly.

"I'm ready."

"Fine."

He silently pointed to Chris's place on stage and then stepped back. He looked to Lisa and then nodded his head for her to begin.

She spoke her lines in a clear but quivering voice.

"Good my lord,
"How does your honor for this many a
day?"

She then waited for Chris to speak, but he just stood there gazing intently at her. His face cold and tight.

"Chris," Caldwell called out. "Say your lines."

But still Chris did not move.

"Chris."

108

He just stood there gazing at her.

"Give him the lines again, Lisa," Caldwell said.

She hesitated.

"Do it."

She began to speak again.

"Good my lord..."

Then she paused and seemed to tremble.

"Lisa," Caldwell called out. "Continue."

She nodded and finished her speech.

"How does your honor for this many a day?"

Chris walked grimly toward Lisa and then spoke.

"Are you honest, Ophelia?"

"Those are not the lines, Chris," Caldwell said. "You're jumping the lines. Let me give them to you."

But Chris waved him away and moved closer to Lisa and then spoke again, his voice rising with emotion and anger.

"Are you honest?"

He suddenly reached out and grabbed her hand and held it tight.

"The truth, Ophelia. Speak the truth. What do you know? Whose side are you on? Get thee to a nunnery. Get thee there. Why wouldst thou be a breeder of sinners? To a nunnery, go. The truth. Tell me the truth. You know what was in the note. You signed it. Didn't you?"

"Chris," she said pleadingly.

"Are you honest, Ophelia?" he shouted.

Suddenly he let go of her hand and looked about him dazedly.

"I'm not well," he said in a broken voice. "I'm not well at all."

Then he walked off the stage and out into the night. He heard Lisa calling for him but he continued to walk through the trees till he could no longer hear her voice.

18

He waited till it was midnight, exactly midnight, and the house was still, completely still. Then he quietly slipped out of bed, put a robe about him, felt for the key chain in his pocket, and smiled grimly. Then he stole out of the room and down the staircase, noiselessly.

Then down the next one till he was on the main floor of the house.

The moonlight came through the locked windows and silvered him as he moved along the corridors, the silent corridors, until he came to the heavy door of the trophy room.

He paused to glance about him and saw that all was quiet and empty.

"Good," he whispered.

Then he selected a key from the key chain and put it into the keyhole and turned the key with a delicate motion.

The lock clicked softly and the door opened.

He stood on the threshold, motionless and alert, and then he went into the trophy room, closing the door behind him. The moonlight swept softly through the barred windows and streaked his face with shadows and silver.

He thought of Jamie sitting in the big black leather

chair, the gun in his hand and the cowboy hat on his massive head.

"Fool. Murdering fool."

He moved silently past three glass cases till he came to the fourth. It was set in a corner of the large gleaming room.

He stood there looking into it, surveying the assortment of small handguns. His eyes and silvery face reflected in the glass.

Reflected and distorted till it became a mask to him.

He turned away from the wavering silvery mask because for an instant it had terrified him.

"Christ," he murmured.

Then he caught his breath again and turned back to the case and saw what he wanted. His eyes glistened in triumph.

"Yes," he whispered.

He took another key from his chain and inserted it into the keyhole of the case. He turned the key and opened the case and put his hand in and took out a small gun and held it up.

The barrel glinted with a cold light.

It was a Mauser automatic that Jamie rarely noticed anymore. He had bought it years ago to fill out his collection.

And then lost interest in it.

Chris felt the gun as it lay in the palm of his hand and it was a good feeling. He no longer felt naked and alone. He now had a strong companion. Chris looked over to the big leather chair and he grinned. Then he closed the case and locked it.

"Well, Claudius? Where are you now?" he murmured.

He grinned again at the chair and then turned and walked to a large closet that stood against one of the walls of the room. It was made of metal and had a heavy lock that hung from the handles of its two doors.

Chris took another key from his chain and put it into the keyhole of the lock. He bent over to turn the key and as he did, the door of the trophy room opened, bit by bit, silently, and a figure slid in and then glided into the cover of darkness and stood there gazing across the room at his bent back.

Chris heard and saw nothing.

He straightened up and opened the closet and then searched the shelves till he found the box of cartridges that belonged to the Mauser. And next to it the clip that fitted the gun. He loaded the clip from the box of cartridges, one by one, and then he inserted the clip into the gun.

He let the loaded gun lie in his palm and he smiled again.

"Well, Claudius?"

He laughed softly.

Then he gazed at the chair and pointed the gun at it. For an instant, in his fevered imagination he saw Jamie sitting in the chair and looking intently at him.

Chris slowly lowered the gun and the image vanished.

"Christ," he whispered.

He turned back to the closet, his face pale and drawn.

"Christ, save me."

The figure hidden in the pool of darkness bowed its head as if in grief. Outside, the night was still and vast.

The leaves of the trees were motionless. Down at the lake the bench, the stone bench, gleamed in the moonlight.

Chris set the box of cartridges back onto the shelf and into its proper place and closed the doors.

He snapped the heavy lock shut.

He dropped the loaded gun into the pocket of his robe, glanced once more at the big leather chair, and then went to the door of the trophy room.

He opened the door and went out into the corridor. He looked about him searchingly and then locked the door.

He walked slowly to the staircase. His face was now white and grim, but in his eyes was a steady light of cold satisfaction.

"I have it, Claudius," he murmured.

Then he slowly, quietly, began to ascend the staircase. All about him was vast, enveloping silence.

In the trophy room, the figure came out of the darkness and into the silver light. It was Ellen.

She went over to the glass case and looked down at the empty spot where the Mauser had lain.

"No," she said. "No. I can't let it go on."

And then she began to weep.

After a while she unlocked the door, stepped out of the room and into the silent corridor.

The tears were still wet on her agonized face.

Then she locked the door and walked down the corridor, her head bowed. Soon she was weeping again.

Outside the moonlight fell over the huge house, over the dark, sleeping house, with a cold sheet of whiteness.

Down at the lake a figure came out of the trees and slowly sat down on the stone bench.

Sat down and stared out over the still water.

It was Jamie.

19

He was lying in the darkness, his eyes open, thinking, ever thinking, when he glanced at the glowing dial of his clock and saw that it was two o'clock. And it was then that he heard Jamie's footsteps on the staircase.

He reached into his pillowcase for the automatic and then he held it tight in his hand under the covers.

He closed his eyes and pretended that he was asleep, all the time listening for Jamie's footsteps to come closer, ever closer.

Then he heard the big cat glide into the room and then he heard the low, low voice.

"Chris."

He didn't answer.

"Chris."

He opened his eyes and saw the massive figure standing in the moonlight. The long powerful arms hanging loosely at its sides.

The hands gleaming in the moonlight.

The thick fingers half-closed.

Claudius knows, he thought. He knows that you know.

"What is it?"

"Chris, it was empty. I swear to you it was empty."

All the time the hand of Chris was tight over the grip of the automatic. The finger near the trigger.

"So?"

Jamie shook his head, side to side.

"I don't know how the bullet got in there."

Chris was silent, alertly watching every move of the huge form. He watched the gleaming hands most of all, the hands that could suddenly reach out and choke off his life in a raging instant.

"Chris, listen to me."

"I am, Jamie."

"Chris, I don't know how I didn't see it there. Maybe I was a bit too drunk."

"Maybe."

The big head nodded again and again.

"Yes. It was that, Chris. I had too much to drink."

"You had."

"Too much. Too much."

"Okay, Jamie. I'm convinced."

The eyes of his father suddenly glittered and the voice became harsh.

"But you're not."

There was a silence, and then Jamie spoke again. This time his voice was soft and pleading.

"Chris, I got too many things on my mind these days. I don't know what I'm doing half the time."

"Yes, Jamie."

"You understand, don't you?"

"I guess I do."

Jamie moved a step closer.

"Ellen doesn't. She doesn't forgive me."

"Ellen?"

"She's stopped speaking to me."

"Oh."

"She won't even let me in the room anymore. I sleep alone. I'm all alone, Chris. All alone now."

And Chris, looking at the big, massive figure and seeing the anguished eyes, for an instant felt a great pity for the man.

A pity he could not fight down.

His eyes became soft, his hold on the gun relaxed.

"You forgive me. Don't you, Chris?"

He wanted to answer but he couldn't.

"Can't you?"

Still he couldn't answer his father's desperate plea.

"You called me a drunken fool. And I am. I am."

Jamie moved closer.

"You said, Get out of my life. I can't, Chris. I can't."

"You can't," Chris said.

And suddenly all the pity for the man left Chris. And all he could remember was the bullet grazing past him and thudding into the wall.

You can't because of the money I have, my father. You tried to kill me.

Claudius knows. Claudius knows that you know. It's his life or yours.

Chris heard his father's voice.

"You do forgive me. Don't you, Chris? You're my son."

"I'm your son, Jamie."

"My only son."

"Your only son."

"Don't leave me out there all alone. Don't, Chris."

"I won't."

"Please, Chris."

Jamie's voice almost broke. He moved forward and was now at the bed. He leaned over to Chris, his huge arms extended, the hands just grazing Chris's face. A cold terror went through Chris and he moved back to the wall, into the shadows, the gun now clear of the blanket.

Held tight in his right hand.

"Chris."

Jamie's eyes were on his son's shadowed face.

"Chris," he said again.

"Well?"

"Chris, you're scared of me."

117

"Maybe I am."

"Why?"

Chris didn't answer.

"Why?" Jamie asked in a bewildered voice.

Don't you know? Chris wanted to shout at him. But he gazed into his father's eyes with a stony look.

Jamie moved backward and away from the bed.

"I love you, Chris."

"I know."

Jamie stood there, his shadow flaring against the wall, huge and menacing. Yet his face was bewildered and agonized.

"I almost killed you downstairs in the trophy room. I can't sleep. I can't eat. I always think of that, Chris."

Chris sat there against the wall, saying nothing. The gun still held in his hand, pointed at the massive figure.

"I...I only wanted to kiss you, Chris. That's all."

"I understand."

Jamie shook his head sadly.

"But you don't. You don't."

They looked at each other in silence, and then Jamie turned wearily and went out of the room.

Chris sat there against the wall a long time, the gun in his hand.

He wondered if Jamie had seen it.

It was impossible to tell.

Then he got up and went to his desk and searched about in the drawers till he found a key. A key that he had used only once before and that was the night a murderer was loose in the area. The man was caught in the gray morning and Chris put the key back into the drawer where it lay untouched for years.

Now he went to the door of his room, closed it, and then locked it. Then he got back into bed and tried to sleep.

Only toward morning did his eyes finally close.

20

The afternoon was gray and cold when he stopped his car in front of his Aunt Rhoda Bentley's building on upper Fifth Avenue. As he got out and looked up at the towering sleek structure, he thought to himself sardonically, It truly is her building. She owns it and lives in it, in that duplex apartment of some thirty or more rooms. That private art museum of hers.

Lives alone like a reigning duchess and her staff of servants.

The little duchess.

Then he said to himself, as he stood tense and impatient in the upper corridor waiting to be let in, I'm beginning to hate and despise her.

Or is it her money?

Am I beginning to hate money and what it does to people?

Is it that?

Makes savages and murderers out of them.

"Savages," he murmured.

Cannibals.

A father would kill his own son and devour him.

"Chris."

It was Rhoda herself who opened the door for him.

119

She looked at him and then drew him to her and held him and would not let him go.

"Chris. Chris, what is wrong?"

And he could swear that it was his mother speaking and pleading with him. He shivered and pulled himself away from her and went to a chair and sat down.

She came over to him.

"Chris, I cut my trip short to come back here."

"I know that, Rhoda."

"George Ramsey called me."

He looked up at her sharply.

"Ramsey?"

"Yes. He's very disturbed over you. He senses that something is...is..."

She did not go on but just stood there gazing at him.

"Well, that's good to know. Just where does he fit into all this?"

"Fit into what, Chris?"

He was silent.

"Chris," she said softly. "You look so pale and bitter. You frighten me."

"Do I?"

"What is going on? Please tell me."

"Shall I?"

"Please."

He stared coldly and bitterly at her.

"Yes, Rhoda. My dear Aunt Rhoda. Something is wrong," he said. "Damned wrong. And you know well enough what it is."

Her mouth opened wide.

"I?"

"Stop playacting with me."

"Chris."

"This is no theater, Rhoda. It's my life."

She grew pale and began to tremble.

"What are you talking about?"

"I went out to Seaside. I know."

120

"Seaside?"

"Yes. I know everything."

He drew out the white envelope from his inner pocket and held it out to her.

"What is this, Chris?"

"Don't tell me you don't recognize this envelope," he said harshly.

"I don't."

"Take it, Rhoda."

She took the envelope and stared at it. And then at him bewilderedly.

"I never saw this before, Chris. Never."

"Open it and read the letter."

She hesitated.

"But..."

"Don't act with me, Rhoda."

"Chris, I..."

"Open it," he shouted and grabbed her arm.

"Chris."

And he saw that she was fearful of him. He thought to himself, I've never seen this look on her face before. Never in all my life.

She is afraid that I will harm her.

"Please."

He let go of her arm.

"Read it," he commanded. "You know every word in it."

She shook her head.

"I tell you, Chris, I don't..."

"Rhoda," he cut in angrily.

"Yes, Chris," she said in a low, meek voice.

He watched her intently as she took out the letter and read it. He saw her hands shake, and the letter almost slipped from her grasp.

"Your mother was murdered," she said and did not look at him.

"That's what it says."

"Murdered?"

The letter now dropped from her limp fingers to

the floor. He let it lie there, white against the dull green of the rug. His eyes were on her, never wavering.

When he spoke, his voice was cold and cruel.

"Well, Rhoda?"

She was silent. She went slowly to a chair and sat down. There was a dazed look on her delicate white face.

Again he thought of his mother.

He had dreamed of her, standing before him, dreamed of her early in the morning just as the sun was coming into the room...her face dripping with streamlets of bright blood, her mouth open wide in a silent scream...

"Where did you get this letter?"

"Rhoda," he said sharply, "I told you to stop acting."

"Chris."

"Stop it."

"I'm not acting."

"You are. You'll soon ask me who sent me this letter. Won't you?"

"Do you know?"

"Yes. I know."

"Who is it?"

He looked squarely at her.

"You, Rhoda."

She shook violently and then rose from her chair. "Me?"

"Yes, Rhoda. You sent me the letter."

"Never."

He rose and faced her.

"Damn it, Rhoda, I drove out to Seaside. That's where the letter came from."

"Seaside?"

"You were there. You mailed the letter from there."

She held out her hands to him desperately. The same way his mother had held out her hands to him in the terrifying dream.

"Chris, I haven't been in Seaside in many years."

He shook his head fiercely.

"Rhoda, I spoke to the man in the post office."

"What man?"

"He remembered you. He described you. You were there."

"Never. I tell you, never."

His voice rose.

"Your car. One of your cars, my little duchess. The gray Mercedes."

"What about it?"

"He described it to me, Rhoda."

"What?"

"Yes. Yes."

She came close to him. Just as his mother had done in the dream, and he felt himself go cold all over.

He waited for droplets of shining blood to appear on her face.

"Chris, these are lies. Absolute lies."

"Are they?"

"Someone is playing a ghastly joke on you."

He turned away from the memory of the dream and his voice became harsh and cruel.

"It's not a joke, Rhoda. Not when it means my life. Not when it means the murder of my mother."

"Murder? Chris, this is not so."

"It is. And you know it."

"Chris, I was there when Marian died."

"Were you?" he asked savagely.

"It was a peaceful death."

"Was it?"

"Yes. Yes. She suffered terribly for days. And then on the last day she fell into a quiet sleep and died."

"Into a quiet sleep."

"Yes."

"And that is how it happened?"

"That is exactly how it happened."

"You lie, Rhoda," he said.

"No. No."

"Where was my father?"

"Jamie?"

"Where was he, Rhoda?"

"Why do you ask that?"

He paused and gazed at her and when he spoke his voice was very quiet. Quiet and controlled.

"Because he killed her."

"What?" she whispered.

"Killed her for the money he needed. And after her death he got it."

She looked at him and shook her head bewilderedly.

"Chris, what has come over you?"

"And now he needs more money. And so he will kill me."

She stared at him, unable to speak.

"Rhoda, don't make me despise you," he said.

She moved closer to him.

"Listen to me, Chris. Please listen."

"No."

"Chris, your father has many, many faults. And you know well enough what I think of him. But murder?"

"I said murder."

"Chris, you frighten me. You need help."

"Yes, Rhoda. I need help," he said softly.

"To ever think a thing like that of Jamie Gordon."

"It's terrible, isn't it?"

"He's your father, Chris. Your father."

"Yes. He's my father."

Suddenly he moved away from her and lashed out. All of his agony and bitterness was in his voice.

"And you're my beloved aunt. And you're lying to me. You're scared of him and you're lying to me. He did kill my mother and you know it too well. That's why you sent the letter to me. But there's no way of proving the murder. And now he's out to kill me. And there'll be no way of proving that when he does kill me. He's a cat. He lands on his feet. Like all cats do."

"Chris. Chris, please..."

"Lies. Lies, Rhoda. The world is full of madness and lies these days. That damned murderer and villain. A king of shreds and patches. Let him follow my mother!"

He turned to go but she put herself before him.

"Chris, stay here with me. Please. Don't go back to that house."

He pushed her away from him and shouted:

"You're a coward, Rhoda. You love me, but you're a coward. You love me and you'll write a letter to warn me but you're a coward. The world is full of cowards these days. Let them all blow themselves up in one atomic storm. They're a race of vermin."

"Chris..."

"Vermin!"

"Chris, wait."

"Good-bye, Rhoda."

"Please."

He shook his head grimly.

"You're a coward. A damned coward."

He opened the door and walked out into the corridor. He knew that she had followed him out and was now standing and watching him, silent and pale.

But he did not turn to her.

Then the elevator came and he stepped in and the doors closed on her. The last thing he saw was her anguished face.

We are through forever, Rhoda, he thought. You'll have to give your beautiful Renoir painting to someone else.

You'll have to find yourself another nephew.

Someone who'll love you as I did and someone you can love as you did me, once, Rhoda.

Nephews are hard to find these days, my aunt. Very hard. Especially at your age.

He began to laugh silently, bitterly.

When he got outside the late afternoon had turned dark and rainy. He turned away from the building, forgetting about his car, and began to walk aimlessly.

The rain came down upon him and yet he walked on, block after block. He turned down a side street, lined with wet, gleaming trees, and it was then, at that instant, that he became aware that someone was following him.

He swung about and peered into the dimness.

A figure moved quickly out of the circle of lamplight and into the cover of a large tree.

He could see the shadow long on the pavement.

He walked on and then abruptly turned again.

There was no one behind him now.

Only the falling rain.

But he could swear that the figure was that of George Ramsey.

21

"Stop it. Stop it at once," Caldwell cried out.

He jumped between Hamlet and Claudius, his face white and tense. The rest of the cast stood about them silently.

"Chris, you are much too violent. You acted as if you really wanted to kill Claudius."

Chris looked down at the rapier in his hand and didn't speak.

"There is a line between theater and reality. And you were crossing it."

Yes, Chris thought with chill fear, I was crossing it. I never should have come to the rehearsal. I never should have let Mr. Caldwell talk me into it. Especially to do this scene.

The scene where the dying Hamlet springs on Claudius and kills him.

"Much too violent, Chris."

He's right. I did want to kill Claudius. It was Jamie I saw there. My dear father Jamie.

His violence has come into me and taken over my being.

I am the true son of Jamie Gordon. The son of a murderer who will soon become a murderer himself.

Chris, is there any other way out? Is there?

He heard Caldwell's voice come to him, and it was now soft and sympathetic.

"Chris, let's try to do the scene over."

Chris looked up at him and silently shook his head.

"Just once more, Chris."

"I don't think so, Mr. Caldwell."

"But we're opening this Saturday night."

"I know."

"You're doing fine. Just a little more work."

"I'm sorry. But I...I..."

In the background he could see the face of Lisa. And he felt that she already knew what he was about to say.

There were tears in her eyes.

"I'm sorry," he said again. "But I can't go on."

"What do you mean?"

"I just can't do the play."

"But, Chris, this means there won't be any performance."

"I know."

Caldwell stared at him, his lips open wide.

"I just can't make it any longer," Chris said.

Then he turned and walked off the silent stage.

22

He was sitting out on the terrace, looking down to the distant lake, the long evening slowly coming in.

He took the gun out of his pocket and stared at it. The pink light glinted off its hard metal.

His hand closed about the grip and then suddenly loosed its hold.

I can't kill him, he said to himself wearily. I just can't do it. The hell with it. Let him kill me. If that's how it is to be.

Let Claudius win for a change.

He put the gun back into his pocket and then he got up and went to the bar and mixed himself a drink.

He walked back to his chair, his footsteps sharp on the flagstones, and then he sat down again, sipping his drink and thinking, ever thinking, and then he became aware that Ellen had come out onto the terrace and was standing gazing at him.

He turned to her and there was a hauntingly tender look in her eyes.

"Chris," she said gently.

She came over to him and then slowly sat down. He waited for her to speak.

"I'm leaving him," she said.

Somehow it didn't surprise him. As if he knew that it was inevitable.

"I'm leaving him now, Chris. For good. I'm packed and ready to go. I'm scared of him."

"Scared?" he asked softly.

"Yes. He almost hit me last night."

"Oh."

"Chris, he did know there was a bullet in the gun."

"Yes," Chris whispered.

"He knew."

The evening stillness hovered about them. Then she spoke again.

"I told him that and he grabbed me and...Chris, get away from him. He's out of his mind these days."

Chris sipped his drink and stared down to the lake. He thought of his mother sitting alone on the stone bench. Waiting for her death to be avenged.

Then he heard Ellen's bitter and despairing voice.

"He doesn't love you, Chris. He doesn't love anybody. He cares for himself and only himself."

"Yes," Chris said.

"He destroys everything and everybody he touches."

Chris turned to her.

"My mother?"

She was silent. But he could see the truth deep in those large brown eyes.

"He told you, didn't he? He must've told you."

She got up and started to move away from him.

"I don't know what you're talking about."

He rose.

"But you do, Ellen."

"No."

"Ellen, he killed her."

"Killed?"

"Yes. That is the word I used."

She stood there staring at him and then she shrugged her shoulders hopelessly.

"You know, Ellen. Or you've guessed the truth. Tell me."

"Nobody ever knows the truth about Jamie," she

130

finally said. "And even if they did they would never tell."

"Even if they did," Chris murmured.

"Yes. Like your Aunt Rhoda, for instance."

"Rhoda? What do you mean?"

A cold smile came over Ellen's face and it made her look cruel and ugly to him. There's hate in you, Ellen, he thought. Deep, deep hatred. I never saw that in you before.

"Do you know why she never married?"

"No."

"Because she fell in love with a man who did not love her. She still loves him to this day."

Chris waited.

"The man is your father. Jamie Gordon."

23

So Rhoda lied to him. She did know the truth.

He wrote a note and he left it on the terrace bar, propped up against Jamie's bottle of Scotch.

> Jamie,
>   Ellen has gone. There is something I have to tell you. I'm down at the lake. By the stone bench.
>
> Chris

Then he went down to the lake and into the cluster of trees that stood close to the stone bench. And he waited there, while the evening shadows softly and slowly lengthened and the water on the lake reddened till he was certain it would turn to the color of dark blood.

Soon he heard Jamie come down through the trees and then out into the clearing and walk slowly to the bench and stand there, massive and huge.

Chris moved stealthily out from the cover of the trees, his gun held tight in his right hand.

"I'm here, Jamie," he said quietly.

Jamie turned around, a smile in his eyes, and then he saw the gun.

"Chris, what the hell...?"

"Sit down, Jamie," Chris said gently.

"Chris."

"Sit down and let's talk a minute."

"I don't get this."

"You will."

Chris leveled the gun and Jamie slowly sat down.

"Good."

Chris came closer to the man, but out of his powerful reach. The gun tight in his hand.

"It's you or me now, Jamie," he said.

"I don't follow you."

"You will. Believe me, you will."

"Chris, for Christ's sake, I'm your father. What's the gun for?"

"You're my father, all right. Yes, Claudius, you're my father."

"Claudius?"

Chris laughed, a low bitter laugh.

"You always said, Life is a game. It's really a stage play. You're King Claudius and I'm Prince Hamlet."

"Chris, what the hell is this all about?"

"You're putting on a good act, Jamie. Why didn't you ever go into the theater? You would have been a star."

"Chris, I..."

He started to rise from the bench and Chris aimed the gun over Jamie's shoulder and into the lake. He squeezed the trigger.

The sound shattered the silence. The echoes finally died away.

"I shoot pretty good, don't I, Jamie? You taught me well."

Jamie's face was white as he sank down onto the bench.

"It's the end of the road for you, Jamie," Chris said. "The bitter end."

A breeze rustled the leaves of the trees and he saw a lock of Jamie's black hair fall out of place and over the massive forehead, and he spoke.

"You murdered my mother, didn't you, Jamie?"

"What?"

Chris slowly, slowly raised the gun and pointed it at the head of his father.

"For her money."

Jamie couldn't speak.

"And now you would murder me. For my money."

"Chris, listen to me."

Chris shook his head.

"No."

"Please listen."

"The game is over, Jamie. And you've lost this time."

The finger tightened over the trigger.

"Chris," Jamie said. "I did kill Marian. I did."

"Then you deserve to die, don't you?"

There were beads of sweat on his father's forehead and as he gazed at them he thought of drops of blood.

"Yes. But before you pull that trigger you must know this. She begged me to kill her."

"What?"

"Yes."

The gun wavered.

"She had been begging me for days to release her from her pain."

"You're lying."

"I wish to God I was."

Jamie's voice broke and he was silent.

"You're lying," Chris said.

But deep within him he knew that he was hearing the truth.

"I loved her, Chris," Jamie said. "Still love her. As I love you. She was in such terrible pain. She begged me again and again for an overdose to end it all."

He stopped speaking for he couldn't go on.

Out on the lake the water rippled with a red glow.

"I was alone with her and I couldn't stand it anymore. Yes, Chris, I did kill your mother. I did. I did."

He bowed his head and the tears streamed down his face.

"Not for her money. Not for that. Only because I loved her so much. Only that, Chris. Only that."

Chris stood there, looking down at the man, the gun still in his hand. Then he heard his father speak again.

"And now you can pull that trigger and wipe out that memory. Wipe it out once and for all. Because it's always with me."

Chris let the gun drop from his hand to the ground and he turned away from his father.

He looked at the trees, the silent trees, and he felt that he, too, was weeping, weeping within.

But his face was still cold and tight.

"And Rhoda knew that you did it," he said.

Jamie slowly raised his head.

"Rhoda? Why Rhoda?"

Chris turned to his father again.

"She was in love with you. Still is. So she kept the secret."

Jamie stared at him.

"Whoever told you that?"

"Ellen."

"She lied to you, Chris. All the way. Ellen was the only one who knew the truth. I couldn't keep it to myself any longer. I couldn't tell you. So one night...Chris, I had to tell someone."

"So Ellen knew all the time."

And Chris saw once again the cold cruel smile on Ellen's face.

"She knew."

"Then it was Ellen who sent me the letters."

"What letters?"

Chris was silent.

"What letters?" Jamie asked again, and he rose to his full height.

"That made me believe that you killed Mother and were planning to kill me."

Jamie's big hands clenched and then unclenched.

"Ellen," he murmured.

"I don't understand why she did it," Chris said.

"I do," Jamie said grimly.

"It doesn't matter now. She's gone."

Jamie shook his head.

"She's not. She's still in the house."

24

He knocked on Ellen's door, a soft, faltering knock. He really did not want to go in and face her.

"It's Chris," he said.

She opened the door and he walked into the room. She had not yet turned on the lights and the evening shadows lay in the corners of the room.

"I thought you were leaving," he said.

Her face was pale and taut. Her eyes were large and he saw fear and agony in them. Her hands twitched.

He couldn't help it but his heart went out to her.

"I...I figured I'd wait around," she said in a low voice.

"To see what happened, Ellen?"

"What do you mean?"

"To see if I killed Jamie?"

She trembled and didn't speak.

"I did. You must have heard the shot."

"Chris."

She stepped back from him, back, till she was in one of the shadowy corners. And it was then that Jamie came into the room, huge and menacing.

She stifled a cry when she saw him.

"Tell him, Ellen. Tell him the truth."

He slowly advanced on her. She moved back into

the corner, her face ashen gray, her eyes large and staring.

"Jamie. Leave her alone," Chris cried out.

Jamie grabbed Ellen and flung her onto a sofa.

"I'll break every bone in your body, Ellen. Tell him the truth."

She looked up at him and then bowed her head.

"Tell him," Jamie shouted.

"I wanted you to kill Jamie," she said to Chris in a flat, toneless voice.

"Why?" he asked.

She looked at Chris and was silent.

"She wanted you to kill me. Or me to kill you," Jamie said. "It didn't matter. Did it, Ellen?"

"No," she whispered.

Jamie moved a step and towered over her and she shivered and turned fearfully away from him.

"The trophy room," he said. "You put the bullet into the gun, didn't you?"

She nodded silently.

"If I had killed Chris you would have told the police that it was not an accident. You would have lied. You would have said that I deliberately killed him for his money. Wouldn't you?"

"Why, Ellen?" Chris asked again.

"The syndicate got to her. To get me out of the way. They bought her off. How much did they promise you, Ellen? A million?"

He grabbed her arm and held it tight. This time she did not try to struggle out of his grasp. She raised her face to him and her eyes were hard and defiant.

"They wanted to buy you out. You didn't want to. They decided to rub you out. One way or another. You were too much of a celebrity to be knocked off, so they..."

"So they decided that my son was to be the hit man," he cut in savagely. "Make him believe that I murdered his mother and was about to murder him. So he kills me and the job is done."

"Yes, Jamie."

"And all the time I didn't know what was going on. All the time you were making Chris into a time bomb. Till he was ready to kill me and wreck his life. All for the lousy, stinking money."

"All for that," she said, and Chris saw how much she hated Jamie. And he wondered if she had ever loved Jamie.

"You filthy louse," Jamie shouted.

He pulled her up and his hands went to her throat.

"Chris," she screamed.

Chris sprang between them.

"Jamie," he cried out. "Jamie, let her go."

"I'll kill her."

"No, Jamie, no. One death is enough," he said.

Jamie turned to Chris and their eyes met and then he slowly relaxed his hold on Ellen. She sank to the floor on her knees. He stood there looking down at her and then he turned and went out of the room.

Chris bent down and helped her to her feet. She stood there swaying, and then she put her head on his chest.

He put his arms about her protectingly.

"Why, Ellen?"

He felt his very soul was in those words.

"Why?" he asked again.

Still she would not meet his anguished eyes.

"I tried to love him," she said. "But he wouldn't let me. He never stopped loving your mother. And so I began to hate him."

She moved away from him and into the shadows.

"I thought you cared for me," he said. "Was that also a lie?"

She raised her head and gazed at him and now there were large tears in her brown eyes.

"Never, Chris. Never."

"Then why? Why did you do it?"

"When you're older you'll understand. Older and dirtier."

"Tell me."

She shook her head and let the tears fall down her cheeks.

"You always had money, Chris. Always and always and always. You'll never understand. Never."

"But I will, Ellen. I'm trying to."

She came close to him.

"Chris. Chris, I tried to get out of it. I saw how much I really cared for you. But they wouldn't let me. They threatened to kill me if I didn't go along with them. Now do you understand?"

"No," he said.

Then he left her alone, standing in the shadows, lost, forever lost.

25

He went out to the terrace. The sun was high in a clear and cloudless sky. The green leaves of the trees flickered in a gentle breeze. Down on the lake the water was smooth and golden.

He stood there and then he turned away from the view and saw his father sitting on another part of the terrace. He was hunched in a chair, his bottle near him, a bleak look on his large face.

Chris walked over and sat down by him.

"Jamie," he said.

The big man didn't seem to hear him.

"Jamie," he said again.

"Hello, Chris."

It was a murmur, no more than that. And Chris looked at his father and saw how lonely and alone he was.

Beneath it all, so lonely and alone.

And that's how it's always been with him, he thought. I never really got to know him.

"Want a drink?"

"No, Jamie."

"Mind if I take one?"

"Go ahead."

But Jamie didn't take his drink. He just sat there, looking away from Chris and into the bleak distance.

"It's third and long, Chris," Jamie suddenly said, still not looking at his son. "So damned long."

"I know," Chris said.

"Third and long. I'll never make it."

"Think so?"

"I know so."

There was a silence.

"We'll make it, Jamie," Chris said.

Jamie slowly turned to him.

"We?"

"Yes, Jamie," Chris said. "We."

Then he reached out and put his hand gently on the big man's shoulder.

Gently and tenderly.

JAY BENNETT has won, in two successive years, The Mystery Writers of America's Award for the "best juvenile mystery." The author of many suspense novels for young adults, Mr. Bennett has also written successful adult novels, stage plays, and radio and television scripts.

Mr. Bennett's professed aim in his young adult novels (that have sold over a million and a half copies) is "to write honest books that speak about violent times...but throughout the books, and in every word I write, there is a cry against violence."